FACTUAL **FICTION**

An Anthology

Shmuel **Shimshoni**

PARTRIDGE
A Penguin Random House Company

To order additional copies of this book, contact
Toll Free 800 101 2657 (Singapore)
Toll Free 1 800 81 7340 (Malaysia)
orders.singapore@partridgepublishing.com

www.partridgepublishing.com/singapore

Dear reader:

As much as imaginary tales are referred to as fiction much fact is intertwined within them. And as much as reality is considered to be entirely accurate the human mind cannot write creatively without embellishing some of the facts.

Each individual may observe an identical scene from a different angle that cannot be exactly what someone other than himself sees.

Therefore the seven stories incorporated in this volume, though fictionalized, probably do possess some truisms. As well, it is virtually impossible, within a world that is populated by several billions of people not to have some character that closely resembles someone or other within these stories.

It is hoped that this book will reach people on all parts of the globe. Therefore, if for some reason one of you readers might feel that you are portrayed in some insulting manner in any one of these tales that is a Heaven-sent coincidence. I accept the blame and wish you will accept my sincere apologies.

Then again if that coincidence portrays you in a positive manner I hope you appreciate it, brag about it to help sell a few more copies to your friends and neighbors.

Shmuel Shimshoni (author)

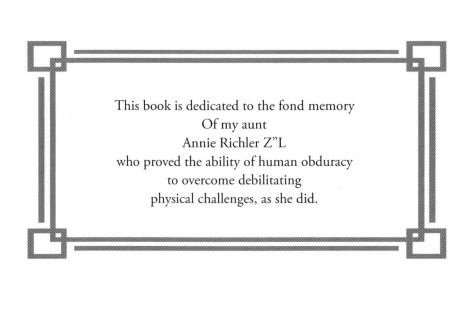

This book is dedicated to the fond memory
Of my aunt
Annie Richler Z"L
who proved the ability of human obduracy
to overcome debilitating
physical challenges, as she did.

CONTENTS

* These two stories have been borrowed from my earlier book
"No Alternative"
and reformatted for inclusion into this book.
By the author.
Shmuel Shimshoni

UNDERSTANDING THE "AGE" SUFFIX

Speaking a "tongue" ("langue" in French) is referred to
in English as conversing in a langu**age**.
As well, we are all quite well aware that:
A number of bags are called bagg**age**,
When one lugs bagg**age** they are carrying lugg**age**,
When items are carted, the activity is called cart**age**.
One who is occupied by rhythmically passing a threaded needle back
and forth, through layers of varied thicknesses and shaped fabrics with a
fluid motion may be referred to as a sewer.
By following a deliberately preplanned continuous straight or curved
line, effectively joining these materials together, clothing is produced by
a sewer, the resulting garments must thence be called
SEW**AGE**.
And since attire is also referred to as garb, the final solid result of those
fluid motions described above, may be referred to as
GARB**AGE**.

AN IMPULSIVE COMPULSION

(It happened during the night of 26/27:03:2000)
Shmuel Shimshoni

I was, making my way up the steep incline. Stretching upwards like a seemingly endless knoll, with horizontally equidistant ranges of stones, row upon row of rocks, laid, one upon the other, each layer set back from the lower one with uncanny precision. Not shapeless boulders or little stones. But elongated stonework that seemed to have been arranged as a very wide staircase. So deep as not to accommodate two strides at a time, but still quite well placed. The stones were rounded off, not only at the corners, but along the length of their edges as well, and stretching off into the distance, both to the right and to the left. I guess I was so engrossed in the ascent that I paid little, if no, serious attention to the width of these stairs. But that they were extremely wide, of that I'm certain.

While I still remember all the intricate details, even after nearly a whole week, I decided to record this spooky episode in my life. Who knows, I might yet meet up with such a site in real life, if such a place really exists on this world. After all I still have plenty of good years to wander around here. At least now I have something to keep on looking for.

I don't remember how it came into to be my hands, but I distinctly remember trying to stuff a large ball of twine into my pocket. In thinking back, it seemed a futile thing to do. To stuff a tightly wound huge ball of string, of about anywhere from fifteen to twenty centimeters in diameter, into a normal pants' pocket. The string was not cotton. Nor was it jute. It was made of plastic fibers, the type in common use today to tie up packages. It was a ball of twine that had been hand wound, of string that

1

was not new. It had already been used before. I know, because it bore plenty of kinks and knots.

Though I was scrambling up the steep "stair case" at a very fast pace. I don't remember becoming winded at all. I just kept on going, being drawn to the summit, I thought to myself, if one actually existed. Eventually the hill began flattening out and the flight of steps here, were of a different type. The rounded steps were behind me, and those before me were flat with sharp edges. They had been identical in spacing, between the risers, just as the ones lower down on the hill. Though the steps here were not smooth, their edges were not rounded. As well, each rock was much longer than the rounded ones had been for most of the way up. As if the other ones had been very long, and were broken, but still very smooth and rounded. The difference was noticeable and distinct. Whoever built this set of steps was a highly meticulous craftsman, an expert stonemason.

I'll probably never know how I got to be there, and neither will any other living soul. Of that I'm certain.

After all this time I'm still perturbed that I'll probably never find out how I got to be where I was at that time. But when I reflect upon it in retrospect, I'm somewhat relieved. That should be the most serious worry that I ever have to endure. After all, it was a remarkable adventure. This was an event that I don't expect to ever experience again. Not for the rest of my life. But who knows! Every day comes with unexpected wonders.

Suddenly an individual appeared from behind and handed me the ball of twine that I had unconsciously dropped some way back down the hill. I thanked him and when examining the ball of string, I found that some of the outer layers of the string had unwound itself from its outer surface. Not an "end", but a loop of twine. While continuing upwards without pausing, I attempted to rewind the loose string onto the ball.

The scene was so strange, yet in some way so familiar that I didn't even pay attention whether it was day or night, at the time. How did I ever get there?

Boy! If I was clambering up the mountain as quickly as I was, this guy must have been flying.

I was just about to ask the man where the place was, that I was being drawn towards when he disappeared from my line of sight. The vision of an unusual framework that seemed somewhat familiar appeared in the distance. It was definitely man made, of smooth concrete, its gray color was still original, and unusually clean. But how could I really be so sure? It was definitely night-time and no lights were anywhere in the vicinity, yet I saw that the framework was rectangular. Easily three times as high as it was wide, and the cross-section of each of its four sided border was perfectly square. Between the top and bottom rails were a number of conical columns that did not reach from top to bottom, but some were standing upright perpendicular to the bottom rail, while others were suspended at right angles from the top rail, non meeting another. They were definitely not in any way equidistant one from another; neither did they signify any specific design. Not even in any obvious interrelation one to another. For example, in one part towards the left, were three such columns close to each other, hanging from the upper rail, then to the right, one such column grew in suspension from the top rail, while in the middle, and from the bottom rail, rose, in a sort of hodge-podge arrangement of additional columns. But none even close to uniting with a counterpart.

I was still following the general path of the man, who had passed me, while still attempting to deal with the bit of unraveled twine from the ball he had returned to me. I managed to catch a momentary glimpse of his right shoulder when he suddenly disappeared again, directly behind that strange artifice at the top of what proved to be a long descending staircase towards the right.

As I reached, just past the, very much out of place, sculpture, my eyes tried to follow the stranger. He was on his way down a very steep, narrow staircase that had been burrowed into the rocky terrain. The flight of steps was lit by the blinding glare of a few bare electric bulbs and I could discern that he had made an abrupt left turn, disappearing from my view again, till I also reached that turn myself. Ahead staircase narrowed perceptibly and was just as precipitous. Following him for awhile, I lost him again when another man suddenly came into view. This one directly facing me was ascending. The staircase being so constricted, I was unsure about how he planned to pass me as I was on my way down with no obvious passing space. As I progressed, I discerned that he had stopped and paused at one point. The steps themselves seemed to have had reached their end, and I found myself walking over a deep canyon with my legs stretched out sideways, and making my way on two protruding concrete extrusions on either side of what appeared to be an abyss. Then I observed that the one who had hesitated was now once again approaching in my direction, where he nonchalantly walked up an incline under my outstretched legs, and continued up the stairs that I had just recently descended.

While I was concerned with this surprising and complex passing maneuver, my first acquaintance, who had returned my ball of twine disappeared, from my sight once more. I wondered where he had gone to now. After shuffling foreword another couple of steps, out on these protruding extrusions, I sought to find how the other man had been able to descend, what appeared to be a long deep narrow recess. Reflecting from the glow of the electric lights dimmed by a mist that arose from the depths, I noticed that there were a series of shallow ridges, seemingly embossed and protruding from long wooden, varnished boards to my right and to my left. The flanges were straight, but neither horizontally, nor vertical; equally spaced one from another on the diagonal, one above the other. On both sides of this plank were handrails as well, in order to facilitate the ascent maneuver, for anybody who wished to get, out of this huge hole in the ground. I didn't remember ever seeing such an arrangement, nor had I ever imagined such a thing. It was awfully bizarre, but that's what I saw so vividly. A truly unbelievable adventure, I mused to myself.

But suddenly I reached the end of those horizontal concrete projections and the first individual was still out of sight. Where could he have, so completely, disappeared to? Aha! So there's still a lower level to this labyrinth. And way down there, the light was a much stronger. Now I could make out the pole to my left. I guessed that this was the only safe way to get down there, by gripping the pole somewhat loosely, and breaking my descent by pressing my feet sideways, against the smooth sides of the walls on either side of me, With such a maneuver I was able to control the velocity of my descent.

The sight that greeted me, just as my eyes cleared the ceiling of the lower level, revealed a very well illuminated enormous chamber with an unusually large number of tiny partitions and separated one from another by low panels, each one containing a small table and a single occupied chair. Like one would observe in a huge office.

The thought that permeated my mind at that moment was, and it was just then that I realized why that odd-looking sculpture next to the staircase at the top of the mountain looked so familiar. Though I had never seen such a sight, somewhere in my subconscious mind such a structure had, at one time, been seared into my memory. It must have been during some dream or even possibly some period in my existence, previous to my present reincarnation. I can't, for the life me, be certain.

Then again it just might have been only in a dream. One of those dreams that one is not supposed to remember upon awakening.

I decided to silently explore this vast underground vault where so many individuals were silently, each doing his (or her) job, or whatever occupied them. Nobody wandered about, they were virtuously all occupied. Every single one, without exception, was silently occupying his minuscule cubicles, each one, all alone. Not a sound could be heard. Nobody was speaking. Not even humming. No music no sound of clicking keyboards, not even the ticking of a clock could be heard in this unusual silence. Though the entire enterprise was underground, the temperature was unusually comfortable, without the aid of fans or air conditioning. Not even the sound of a scrape of a shoe on the stone floor. No voices and no echoes. In a way it was pleasantly eerie.

In my wanderings up and own the aisles I was not accosted in any way. It was as if I was totally invisible and not in existence. I chanced to peek into some of the booths and was surprised to see, that though a screen was perched upon each table, there was not even one keyboard, speaker, microphone, camera or mouse in front of any of those people. Come to think about it, they were all male. Not one single woman among the, how many thousands, I wouldn't even venture to guess. In fact the screens were not computers. They were television displays. The men were each facing their individual screens, contemplating the constantly shifting texts and graphics that were playing before them. Another strange thing was that over each one of the TV screens was a mirror, that envisioned was placed there so that an individual could discern who might be behind him without swiveling around, and possibly missing any part of the seemingly intriguing message displayed in front of him. Though the scene was so serene, a keen sense of dynamics was totally evident.

I abruptly stopped in my tracks while passing one of those little stalls. An uncontrollable shiver gripped me because of what I saw reflected in the kittle mirror on the wall. This was a face that perfectly resembled my brother Murph who had disappeared some twenty years ago. The person sitting with his back to me also happened to glance at the mirror simultaneously. For the first time, in the many hours of my wandering around, I heard a clear whisper. The man before me just said one short sentence, "Shim, is that really you?"

I was in shock. How is it possible? My older bother Murph had just abruptly disappeared. Nobody knew how. Nobody had any idea where. And here he is quietly sitting right in front of me. Not showing any emotions whatever. Not even getting up, nor turning around. I never would have imagined such a cool reception, never mind after twenty years. Is that the way a long lost brother greets a sibling?

"Murph," I asked, "How in the world did you ever get here? What have you been doing all this time?" He smiled with the grin than was his hallmark for as long as I remembered him and replied, "Shim, you remember that high thick hedge that faced Main Street? The one we passed thousands of times on the way to and from school or work; actually wherever we had to go along Main Street and there was no way to avoid it. That hedge was always beside us. The numerous times I tried to find some kind of break in the hedge that would allow me to explore what was hidden behind it, Then one evening, I don't know for what reason, I performed an unprecedented deed. I leaned back, to allow a couple to pass by on the narrow sidewalk. And found myself leaning further back than I thought was sufficient for that maneuver. Another step back and still another one, until I found that I was not making contact with the resilient hedge. Just a few more steps backwards and before I realized it, I found myself in a well cultivated field and the hedge, now before me was once again became a solid wall of foliage without an opening of any sort in sight. Well, I thought to myself, since I was on the other side of the enclosure I may as well look around and turned around to see what I had been so curious about for as many years as I could remember.

I interrupted his narrative with a question, "Murph, what happened to the deep scar you had on your forehead? You remember how it happened. You were showing off, riding your bike "no hands" and when you smashed into the goal post you went flying onto the grass. That's when you got the moniker, "Murph the Turf"". His brother replied, "Shim, here, they fix up everything. Even that broken tooth is all right now". "But last time we saw you your head was quite bald. Did they fix that up too?" I asked. "You bet they did, and all the other little problems I had. I'm as good as new now," explained Murph. "But getting back to your first question."

"Once I found myself on the well groomed stretch of grass I felt some impulsive urge to continue with my exploration, distancing myself from the hedge. The further I went the more I felt a compulsion to continue, and at an even quicker pace. Something was drawing me further into unknown territory. Then I found a large wooden cube. It must have been at least fifteen centimeters in each dimension, and bent down and picked it up. As soon as it was in my hand I found myself rushing ever so speedily towards some mysterious goal. Without realizing it, I found myself navigating a set of steep stone stairs.

The scene was so strange, yet in some way so familiar that I didn't even pay attention how I ever got there, nor whether it was day or night at the time.

Here I was, making my way up the steep incline. Stretching upwards like a seemingly endless knoll, with horizontally equidistant ranges of stones, row upon row of rocks, laid, one upon the other, each layer set back from the lower one with uncanny precision. Not shapeless boulders or little stones. But elongated stonework that seemed to have been arranged as a very wide staircase. So deep as not to accommodate two stairs at a time, but still quite well placed. The stones were rounded off, not only at the corners, but along the length of their edges as well, and stretching off into the distance, both to the right and to the left. I guess I was so engrossed in the ascent that I paid little, if no, serious attention to the width of these stairs. But that they were extremely wide, of that I'm certain.

I distinctly remember unsuccessful trying to stuff the large wooden cube into my pocket. In retrospect, it seemed a futile thing to do. To stuff a huge piece of wood of about fifteen centimeters in every dimension, into a normal pant pocket. It was not a smooth block of wood. It had already been knocked around a lot and was quite a bit distressed. I know, because it bore plenty of dreadful marks and broken corners. I'm not certain if it had ever been treated to a coat of paint upon its surface.

Though I was scrambling up the steep "stair case" at a very fast pace. I don't remember becoming winded at all. I just kept on going, being drawn to the summit, if one actually existed. Eventually the hill began level out, and the flight of steps here were of a different type. The rounded steps were behind me, and those before me were flat with sharp edges. They had been identical in spacing, between the risers, just as the ones lower down on the hill. Though the steps here were not smooth, their edges were not rounded. As well, each rock was much longer than the rounded ones had been for most of the way up. As if the other ones had been very long, and were broken, but still very smooth and somewhat beveled. The difference was noticeable and distinct. Whoever built this set of steps was a highly meticulous craftsman, an expert stonemason.

Suddenly an individual appeared from behind and handed me the wooden block that I had unwittingly dropped some way back down the hill. I thanked him and assured myself that this was really the block that I had been carrying up the stairs. While continuing upwards without pausing, I stupidly attempted to continue stuffing it into my normal size pocket.

If I was clambering up the mountain as quickly as I was, this guy must have been soaring.

I was just about to ask him where we were heading for, actually where I was being drawn towards when he disappeared from my line of sight. An unusual framework appeared in the distance. It was definitely man made, out of smooth concrete, its gray color was still original, and unusually clean. But how could I really be so sure? It was definitely night-time and no lights were anywhere in the vicinity, yet I clearly discerned that the framework was rectangular. Easily three times as high as it was wide, and the cross-section of each of its four sided border was perfectly square. Between the top and bottom rails were a number of conical spindles that did not reach from top to bottom, but some were standing upright perpendicular to the bottom rail, while others were suspended at right angles from the top rail, non touching another. They were definitely not in any way equidistant one from another; neither did they signify any specific design. Not even in any obvious interrelation one to another. For example, in one part towards the left were three such spindles close to each other, hanging from the upper rail, then to the right one such spindle grew in suspension from the top rail, while in the middle, and from the bottom rail, rose in a sort of hodge-podge arrangement of additional spindles. But none even close to meeting with a counterpart. Had I not been so intent on keeping that man in my sight I most certainly would have paused to examine this fascinating piece of art.

I was still following the general path of the man, who had passed me, while was still attempting to deal with the cube that he had returned to me. All of a sudden I caught a momentary glimpse of him when he unexpectedly disappeared directly behind that strange artifice at the top of what proved to be a long descending staircase to our right.

In short, that is how I found myself to be where I am right now, and I wouldn't wish to leave, no matter for whatever one might attempt to entice me with."

"Murph", I have another question that I must ask you," said I, his younger brother. "Could you direct me to the men's room? It's been hours since I'm here, and though I don't feel the immediate need right now, you know . . . When one has to go, one has to go".

To this Murph smiled again and replied, "Shim, in this whole place we don't have a men's room. It's not necessary." "Murph, where is the nearest water cooler? Shim, it's not necessary. So when do you eat around here?. Surely you eat sometimes! Don't you?" "Shim I'm sorry that I have to disappoint you, but here we don't have to eat either. As a matter of fact, none of us even have any carnal desires here. Here we neither drink, eat, sleep nor have to relieve ourselves as living beings must. Shim, in case you didn't realize it, you are now in paradise".

I was thunderstruck! "What? Did I really end up in paradise? How did this happen to me? What did I ever do to deserve this kind of life? You mean no more eating, drinking, sleeping or do whatever living creatures desire and were even commanded to do?"

"I'm afraid you're right Shim. You're one of us now. So get used to it. Tell me Shim do you really need a men's room? Or is it only a carry over habit from your yester-life?"

I replied, "OK! Murph, only I never really thought about my physical "needs" like eating as habits that can be dropped if I really wished to. But there's something else I don't understand. Can you clear up the matter concerning the ball of string, and the wooden cube? Is there a rational explanation you can offer me for those silly props?"

This time it was with a slight chuckle, and this time he actually swiveled around to face me. Then Murph began, "You know Shim, that also troubled me as well, and I asked around. Some of the other fellows found unusual items on their way up, such as an over-sized nut and bolt with a stripped thread that refused to advance past a certain point, or a tricky game that didn't work because a piece was missing. All these things were set out for each of us to find, keeping each of us frustratingly occupied so that we wouldn't realize we were being ensnared. This is not a trip that one makes willingly. The transition is too extreme, and though one is worthy any other method of getting him here is hardly possible. Each one of those decoys contains a homing device, and if you remember, as soon as you had it in your hands your acceleration picked up. When you dropped the object you were running on inertia, and when you slowed down the being that followed you returned it so you'd get up to speed again. Once you entered the "down" staircase there's no turning back. The only time one leaves this place is when sent out to perform a task. But very quickly, you get to like it here, even hoping you never have to leave on any special mission."

To this I asked, "But please tell me, you always seemed to enjoy aggravating and insulting everybody. What did you ever do to deserve a place paradise?"

"Well since you asked, and I'll tell you. You remember what we were taught as kids, that the soul returns to earth to take up residence in some human body in order to rectify wrongs that were performed during previous incarnations. Each time that soul is reincarnated a few more defects can and should be rectified. Well, in a previous lifetime I was implanted into the body of a roughneck. We used to enjoy pushing people off the narrow sidewalk into the gutter. It seemed like great fun. But this last time around I was supposed to make good for that transgression. As I stepped back against the solid hedge, when in reality, there would never have even been place for two others to pass by anyway without maneuvering into single-file, that deed cleaned me of the wrongs that I'd been guilty of, and with a perfectly clean slate, I'm quite sure that I'll never have to undergo life in a human being any more." So Shim, what do you say now?" You also must have done some good deed recently. So you're here, in paradise. Better get used to the idea. You'll get to like it.

In a panic, while trying to locate where that entrance/exit staircase was I yelled, "I'm not ready to die yet. I want to go home!"

I returned to a normal form of life when my wife gently poked me awake, with, "Shim! The way you were thrashing around, like you were trying to creep out of a grave. Was that another of your silly dreams about purgatory?" I replied, "No honey. It was worse than Gahanna. Just promise me that you won't walk near that tall hedge on Main Street. I fact, keep away from that side of the street altogether.

Then it suddenly dawned on me, we don't have any thoroughfare in our city called "Main Street". Neither did I ever have a brother called Murph, and being a first-born, I never had an older brother either. So it must have been only a dream, but one I'll never forget, for as long as I live.

One thing I learned that night that I'll always remember, though life on this world may be challenging and even exciting at times, it's definitely more interesting than death in paradise.

ODE TO THE BANK

My bank in not much better in rank,
Than most depositories that bank
The tellers hardly tell,
Especially when, Oh! Oh! There goes the bell.
The manager survives quite well
The message boy doesn't mess around
We're only small investors, and by the pound
My banker hardly takes an interest
in our wishes, needs or any of the rest.
But my reply to their offer is "Rejected!"
When my sizable deposit is detected,
That's when they're prone to propose
"What do you really suppose?"
"You have the right to take a loan."
However, I'm watchful with what I own,
And turn them down with a, "Thank,
But I don't wish, to be **owed to the bank**."

A GRUBBY JOB

Rinnnngggg! Rinnnngggg!!!

"Hello . . . Mom. I was just about to call you."

With an admonishing tone she answered, "Wellll, it's about time. I've been trying to reach you since yesterday. Mike, what's come over you? Every time I called, you just grunted and hung up on me. Is that the way to treat your own mother? And don't tell me Ime I dialed the wrong number. I used the automatic dialer that you set up for me."

"But Mom, I can explain . . ."

"You'd better tell me all about it! What's come over you?"

"Mom. It's a long and complex story."

"I was so offended by your abruptness. I don't know what to say. And I don't like excuses. You owe me an explanation, and it had better be good."

"Dear mom, I really don't know how to begin, but . . ."

"Mike, don't "Dear mom" me. You'd better start at the beginning."

"Nu! I'm waiting."

Gathering my wits I pleaded with her, "Just please don't stop me in the middle. The whole thing started when I realized that my head hurt something terrible. I felt like it was in a tightening clamp. With every step towards my destination the pain became fiercer. The well worn path I was treading had been used by many people but right now nobody was in sight.

My having arrived in this environment that morning from the northeast part of the continent had not prepared me for the extreme arid weather that is the norm in this patch of desert. I would still have to tread less than a quarter of a kilometer of this patch of wasteland till I'd find some shade, never imagining that the sun could be so scorching hot. With each step this blinding headache was becoming more severe. I thought I was certain that I could make those last few hundred meters but a growing anxiety was vying with my normal optimism, that I could make it.

The two heavy paper bags full of groceries from the supermarket were not helping me keep up my normal stride, actually causing me to suffer additional time in the sunshine. Worst of all, not one of the items that I had bought was liquid. Something that would have helped fight off the thirst that was taking its toll on my confidence.

After progressing about another hundred meters I raised my eyes towards the first structures of habitation looming ahead. The houses still seemed to be as far off as when I last glanced at them some time ago. It was not a very encouraging sight, but when I lowered my eyes to the ground again, I found that during those few moments I had veered off the path towards the left. My steps had been so labored for the last quarter of an hour that I hadn't felt the different texture of the ground. That was a bad sign. Was I was losing my coherence? Why didn't I realize I had wandered off the beaten track? The dunes beside the trail were sandy and walking around in soft sand expends more effort.

This was the first time in my entire life that I was experiencing dehydration, and hadn't realized how serious my situation was.

I hadn't even realized at what point I let go of the two bags of groceries, but they just slipped out of my hands, while I plodded along with whatever energy was still available, attempting to approach some shade.

The next thing I knew I was strapped into a gurney, so as not to roll off while the ambulance sped in its way. I was able to move my head to an extent, and when I opened my eyes saw two bags of saline fluid hanging from an overhead hook, feeding liquids directly into my right and left veins located just at my shoulder bones. A medic, standing over me was squeezing one of the saline bags in order to help get the fluids transferred into my system that much more quickly.

I attempted to ask him what happened. How did they find me? But the words that issued from between my dry lips were not even clear to me. He turned to assure me that all would be well, "Just relax, and we'll have you there in less than an hour."

My mind was still functioning, and I thought to myself, "In less than an hour? How far are the hospitals from places of habitation in this part of the country?" But I couldn't put it into words that could be understood.

Another glance at the *medic,* and I was quickly losing confidence. He wasn't wearing even a white shirt. His garb was entirely leisurewear. He was unshaven, and not with a trimmed beard, just a few days' growth of facial hair. What I could make out of his attire proved that he had donned a yellow T-shirt and a pair of tattered looking jeans. From my position I couldn't tell if they were long pants or shorts. But he looked to me a lot less than a medic should. Was I really being driven to a hospital or to some sinister rendezvous?

Trying to analyze what was happening I distinctly remembered that I had arrived at some town in the middle of the desert just after dawn by bus to fulfill a contract, that shouldn't have taken more than a week at most. The trip from the east was entirely uneventful.

No one knew that I had arrived. I hadn't even looked into arranging for living quarters yet. I just checked my luggage at the terminal, and walked the couple of kilometers to the next town after having been told that the shopping center there was much better stocked than the local one. That was quite early in the morning and the heat was not as extreme as the two hour difference had proven to me how the sun could stoke up such a great head of steam in such a short time under desert conditions. No one would know I was missing. Was I being kidnapped? Or snatched as a hostage? As I struggled to free my arms from the tight straps holding me to the stretcher the guy beside me called out to the driver, "Willie, he's awake and attempting to free himself."

"Okay Jake. If he gets too active, you know what to do," replied the driver.

As I attempted to twist around to get a better view of what Willie looked like. I noticed that Jake had snapped open an ampoule of some brownish liquid, filled a syringe and with an experienced flourish injected the tip of a needle into my upper arm. Within moments I was out of it.

When I woke up again I found myself lying on a bed. Nobody else was in a strange room and realized that I was very closely being monitored via a closed-circuit camera, set on a swivel base and a movement detector that would rouse anybody monitoring my every move if I should as much as stir from my present position. One wall of the semi-darkened room held some half a dozen monitors actively showing various scenes. One however, was obviously connected to various parts of my body revealing my physiological functions, heart, pulse, temperature, etc. A clock with a sweep second hand showed the time to be about 23:00 hours.

I had neither eaten nor did I drink for over fifteen hours, but worse than the hunger and thirst was my urgent need to relieve myself. As soon as I sat up on the edge of the bed a voice came over a loudspeaker, "well Mike, so you're awake?" Just don't try to leave the room. Just ask for whatever you want. If it's within reason you'll have it. If you behave yourself, nobody will get hurt."

"Can I have the use of a toilet? Urgently."

I then thought to myself, "How does he know my name? I'm sure I didn't tell any of them."

His reply was quick, "Sure, you'll find one in the right corner of the room. The window there is barred and besides, it's under surveillance, so don't think of escape."

"Would somebody disconnect all these cables that you so thoroughly connected to me?"

"There are only a half a dozen of them, so just detach them by yourself.

"Thank you," I replied somewhat abruptly. "And when I'm finished I'd like something to eat. I'm famished."

The facetious reply asked, "Will you want it with toast?"

I dropped the subject, while making for the bathroom. No sense getting worked-up while they had the upper hand.

As soon as I'd relieved myself and returned to the room, a tray had already been placed upon a small folding table next to a three-legged stool in the center of the room. I guess I'll never know how they got it all together so quickly. Four slices of buttered toast with a couple of eggs, a small jar of plum jam and a cup with a pitcher of hot coffee, along side of which were a few sachets of sugar and a spoon. I noticed the lack of a fork and knife. These guys, might have been the same Jake and Willie who had picked me up from the desert sands? They were very careful, and didn't act or even address me abusively. As a matter of fact, they saved my life. They were in no way abusive. I had no idea where I was, or why I was being held in this kind of place under these conditions. Here I was, being held incognito, yet I didn't question them about the reason and they never intimated that I might be here against my own wishes. Actually we never even discussed it in those terms. But why? Who was I to have them treat me with kid gloves, yet as a prisoner, so far, a willing prisoner? In reality I didn't have any address in this part of the country. Nobody was expecting me in this locale. I work alone without any local contacts and when I finish my inspection I leave as surreptitiously as the way I arrive on these jobs. Nobody would look for me, nor realize that I was missing. But I really wasn't missing. I was just going along with the charade. So far I hadn't been maltreated.

Back in the northeast I lived alone. When I took off, as I had some three days ago nobody noticed and nobody would care if I didn't show up for a couple of weeks, as long as my rent was fully paid-up, as it was now and for the next three months.

Why did I travel by Greyhound? I never did like air travel and wasn't in any rush. My contract had no specific dates involved. As long as I performed my task responsibly, and presented a comprehensive report of my findings, that was all my client wanted. I had performed such services for him in the past and am quite certain that he wouldn't seek the services of anybody else for this kind of project. He knew that I didn't promise to work against any stringent timetable, and the results would be worth the fee agreed upon. Of course along with the fee I was always reimbursed for all and sundry expenses.

Even though the hour was quite late and my having been asleep all day, slumber wouldn't come to me. Along with that, my mind was attempting to sort out the situation I found myself to be in now. I had been treated quite well, but was being kept as a detainee. What did Willie and Jake want from me? My occupation was highly specialized and the field was extremely narrow. These guys were not the kind who would even appreciate what I did for a living. So why deprive me of my liberty?

But then I didn't have an opportunity to ask them, so why should I be surprised that they didn't explain what they wanted of me? I was still wide awake, but at his hour they were probably asleep and wouldn't appreciate being awakened just to satisfy my curiosity, so I let it ride till the morning. And if they would admit that they made a mistake and open the door for me to leave right now at, a glance at the clock-face showed it to be 1:48 am, what would I do? Roam around at this hour, not even knowing from where I was trying to get to an unknown somewhere? Better to leave any discussions till daytime.

I tried to consider the project at hand and how I was to go about getting started as soon as I was out of here. I had all the instruments I'd need wrapped up in my luggage, still stored in the bus terminal. I hope that the key is still in my billfold, and fumbling to reach into my right pants pocket to check it, found that both my right and left pockets had been emptied. Now I had something else to consider. My cell-phone was also missing. Till now I hadn't even considered the value of that phone and how I might have used it to attempt contacting anybody on the outside who would free me from this situation. I now had another thing to worry about. Much of my personal life was recorded in that phone's SIM card, including vital contacts. My mind was mulling over the significance of my personal SIM (**S**ubscriber **I**dentity **M**odule) card. A removable smart card used in all GSM mobile phones as well as UMTS phones, satellite phones and some CDMA phones, it contains a unique ID and an authentication code assigned to me as well as my phone contacts and network-specific data, that was programmed to display custom menus on the phone's display. In the wrong hands my SIM card could prove to be disastrous. And the kind of people who designed this digitally controlled house just might be able to decipher the data entered on that card, and use it to my detriment. Even under normal conditions I wouldn't have been able to fall asleep but now I was really worried.

Tossing and turning on the bed over and over again, though the mattress was not uncomfortable, I still couldn't find a comfortable enough position to drift off into any kind of sleep. All the troubling thoughts wafting through my brain were overbearing and far from relaxing.

I felt an urgent need to drink something and as I sat up on the edge of the bed some motion sensor must have activated a spotlight following my every move, but I didn't head for any door so no alarms were activated. My direction was towards the little table, where I gulped down the rest of the cold coffee that had remained from my late supper. That thick bitter residue would surely prevent me from falling asleep now. Making my way back to the soft, but firm mattress, I was still under surveillance. It was all part of my being held hostage. The clock registered 4:20 am And I knew that if at all, I'd enjoy a short nap at most.

A dazzling sunbeam streaming through a pin-hole gap in the window shade woke me up, and since it was so close to the clock, I was too blinded to make out what time it was. My having been in this region for less than a day, I had no way of my guessing what the time might have been. My attempt to get out of the bed was immediately picked-up by the motion detector. This time I was not bathed by the radiance of a spotlight. Instead a heavy voice greeted me over the speaker, "Good morning sleeping beauty. All rested up now? Are you ready for some breakfast? But first we'll have a little chat, if that's okay with you."

I was still a bit groggy, but managed to reply, "Sure, good morning. But I'd like to get washed up first." Actually having a discussion was something I was aching for since the moment I found myself in this place. I am thankful that my life was probably saved when Willie and Jake picked me up off the arid desert floor, as I was rapidly dehydrating. I am most grateful for that. But why am I being kept in solitary confinement, like some sort of criminal? Who are my benefactors? They don't seem to be a very sociable pair. Not towards me anyway. They're tough but don't seem to be exceedingly rough. A strange breed they are.

I made it to the bathroom and though my clothing was rumpled, at least my body functioned properly. A new tube of toothpaste and a toothbrush, still in its original bubble pack had been placed on the shelf during the night. I opened it, hoping that it was intended for my use. A new bar of soap and a towel, different from the one that was draped over the towel-bar last night, were also provided.

During the few minutes that I had been occupied with my personal grooming, the little table with last night's dishes had been removed, and the bedspread straightened out. Nothing else seems to have been done in the room that I regarded as my prison. In the daylight that was very much diffused, but still quite strong I discerned that one wall was actually a series of doors, six in all, one beside the other, all leading inwards to this room, and none of them had any knob or handle on my side. They all seemed to be controlled from the outside. But while my analytical mind observed that fact, I realized that if no one would be on the outside to control them, while one or more of them would be on the inside, they would have to have some other means of opening any of these doors. So it's possible that it must be done by an electronic wireless control unit. At least one, if not more of those doors would be electronically controlled. Then again if more than one of them was to be electronically controlled, the remote would have to be programmed with a separate code for each lock. While I admired the technology that had been built into this room I sensed an appreciation for the foresight in choosing such a site, wherein to keep someone like me hostage.

With these thoughts rushing through my mind I glanced once again towards the array of monitors on the opposite wall, noticing that no controlling device was evident. No keyboards and no mouses, not even a telephone, though there were a good many sockets where such devices might be plugged in, when they might wish to use them as control terminals. Presently, however they were all impotent.

With a silent but discernable click the third door from the left suddenly swung into the room on well lubricated hinges and a giant of a man filled the entire doorway. For a moment he didn't move. It was neither Jake nor Willie. Though I hadn't really had a good look at either, yesterday, they were not that huge. This one was a new man on the scene.

His voice was audacious but not threatening. As a matter of fact when he introduced himself he might even have been putting on a show of being humorous. While pointing an index finger towards his chest he said, "Hugh—me. Then pointing in my direction he added, And you—Mike?"

Then with a wide grin, he strode into the room, and as the door closed behind him he straddled the three-legged stool, that really hardly looked sturdy enough to support him, but surprisingly didn't buckle from his apparent immense weight.

"Okay, now we know who we are. I'm Hugh and you're Mike. We hardly know much more than that, about each other. Am I correct? Before you get your breakfast, and your attitude will determine what it is going to be, I'd like to have a few answers to some simple questions. Are you with me Mike?"

"Sure. Go ahead and ask. Then I'd like to ask a few questions of my own, if that's okay with you."

"That sounds fair enough, if your answers are satisfactory. I'll start first."

"I have a list of names of some of your conspirators. I want you to tell me whatever you can about each one of them. Who is Flufy Flour?"

I replied, somewhat flustered, "I never knew such a name ever existed. You're surely joking. Aren't you?"

But Hugh came back with another weird name, "And who is Yester Moro?"

"You must be kidding. Where did you ever make up such odd names?"

Hugh continued, shooting out strange sounding names that included, "Yikity Yakity", "Bugsy Mugzy", "Rodem Dodum", Shishy Show", Mumnles Bug", BlewBury Pi", and a few more peculiar names like that. To each and every one, I replied,

"I never could imagine such names, and definitely never met anybody with nicknames like any of those. There's not even one normal name in the whole list you mentioned."

"Well Mike, if that's the best you can do you'll get some breakfast but don't complain about what's in it." Hugh stood up and turned to face the second door from the right. It silently swung open to let him out and without another word he stepped through to the next room. The door swung closed as easily as it had opened.

After a few moments a voice instructed me to enter the bathroom, close the door, count to ten then return to the room. I did as I was instructed. When I returned the little table had been returned with a tray of hot cereal, buttered toast, an egg and a pitcher of cocoa, a cup and a spoon. Again no knife or fork was provided. These guys were really suspicious of me and any capability of my utilizing these utensils to attempt an escape.

As soon as I caught sight of the food I realized that I was hungry and didn't waste much time in beginning to polish off the fare. Though I was thirsty I found it hard to enjoy the cocoa without milk. It was more like trying to drink mud.

My attempts to communicate with any of my captors were rebuffed. It was they who controlled the line of communication. Even if I were to approach any of the doors that all opened inwards, without handles, there was no way I could even attempt to force my way out. The windows had been barred as well so I was at their mercy. At least I knew that they were now at least three of them and they had full surveillance of my every movement.

After having tried to quench my thirst from the contents of the pitcher I remembered that maybe I could wash down the "mud" with plain water, and made for the bathroom. But when I got there I found that the water taps had been removed. Even the toilet tank top had been screwed down to prevent my getting some "clean" water. But how did they make these changes in the bathroom without my sensing their activities? Following a thorough search I found that a, quite well camouflaged sliding door had been fashioned into the wall behind the collapsible shower stall, giving any one of them access and egress whenever they wanted. These guys were very resourceful, and far from friendly.

If this was some kind of punishment for not telling about the strange names that Hugh had read out to me earlier how was I to change course during the next round that was certain to come? Actually there was no way I could do anything till I renewed contact with any of my captors. They were the ones pulling the strings. So I just had to wait. Meanwhile I tried to plan some strategy whereby I would improve my position.

Sure enough after more than an hour had past, the same third door from the left opened and Hugh came lumbering in, silently took his seat and ruffled a sheaf of foolscap sheets while he sought one that he wished to use as a guide, pulled it out of the stack and placed it on top of the pile.

"Okay Mike, let's get to work," were his opening words to this second round. "Have you changed you mind? Are you ready to tell me what you know about those names I read out to you earlier? I have a couple more here, if that will help jog your memory. What about "Riski Wiski?" or "Barum Durum?""

"Look, Hugh. It is understood that the Jewish people are known for answering a question with another question so please let me reply to yours with a Jewish reply. If you're asking me to try and help you solve a problem why don't we both work in that direction together? If you treat me like an adversary we might never get an answer to your problem. If you're serious lets get to work and then I can get out of here and begin working on the project that I'm getting paid to do. So, what do you say?"

Hugh seemed to become upset with my proposal. I guess that's not the way these guys work. Hugh was beginning to show his lack of authority when he said, "I'll have to get authorization for that."

"What kind of authorization do you need to get some nicknames deciphered? By the way who ever though up those silly names anyway? Is it some kind of game you're into?"

Now Hugh was becoming flustered. He had probably never been put on the defensive before, even with his massive build. But slipped up with his facade when he intimated, "Mike, you should know about those words. They were on the SIM card in your cell-phone."

Now it was my turn to be in shock, "My cell-phone?" never in my entire life have I ever heard such combinations of words, like "Yerster Moro" or "Blewbury Pi". Never mind entering them into my cell-phone. Are you sure that you're referring to my phone?"

"That's the one that was found in your left hand pants pocket when you were picked up off the sand in the desert, just outside of Blink, Nevada. There is no way we could have made a mistake about that. Now don't tell me that it isn't your phone!"

"Just to make doubly certain that it is or isn't my phone, would you place a search on that SIM card for my dear mother's phone number? It should be 517-684-4316. Being an only son I doubt that phone number would be on any other cell-phone SIM card in the entire world."

It gave me some sense of pleasure to see that I now had some influence on the proceedings, as Hugh got right up from his stool and left the room to perform that check on the SIM card they was in their possession, suspecting that it was mine.

Within a couple of minutes he was back with an apologetic, yet troubled smile on his lips. "Are you sure you gave me the correct number for your mother? 514 684-4361? There is no such phone number programmed into that card. So how come this phone was in your possession? How come we didn't find any other one? A cell-phone that you could claim as yours?"

"In order for me to reply to that you'll have to fill me in on some facts concerning this search that seems to be so important to you. Who are you and what do you think I know that concerns you and your buddies?"

Hugh was now on the defensive and had to come up with a plausible but reasonable reply if he was going to have me cooperate. He asked, "We only know you as Mike. What is your full name,? What is you occupation? What brings you to these parts? And why did you suddenly appear specifically at this time?"

"I have nothing to hide. My name is Michael Shtearn and I hail from Boston. What do I do for a living? I investigate sewage seepage sources when it leeches the local potable water supply in any region. I have virtually no competition in the field, and traverse the entire continent performing my specialized service. My service fee is high enough to live on comfortably. And I might add that my earnings are clean.

"If you have such a lucrative business, why do you waste your time traveling by Greyhound? You could have saved nearly two days if you made the trip by plane? Or did you think that it would be easier for you to make a get-away than going through airport security?"

"I prefer traveling by bus. That way I get to see the country, besides which it gives me time to work out my next venture. But what exactly did you mean to imply with that expression, "to make a get-away?" What, were you inferring to with that statement?"

Well since you are showing some cooperation, maybe you'll go all the way, and tell me where you stashed the money? We found the locker key that you had in your wallet, but only found some clothing and a few odd instruments in the bag you checked. Where did you hide the cash?"

"Cash??" I asked, incredulity. What cash are you talking about? I usually travel with a few small bills for sundry purchases and credit cards. Why would I pack cash in my luggage?"

"Go on Mike. Don't get smart with me now. You know what I'm talking about. Where's the loot that you carried away from the First National Trust heist."

Well I do have a personal account at the First National Trust bank, but haven't been through their doors for nearly half a year. Payments for my services are usually made via direct transfer by my clients and I follow most of my banking over the internet and withdrawals at convenient ATM's. What makes you think I'm carrying loot from a heist?"

Immediately after a robbery that took place at about half past eleven on Tuesday a call initiated from your cell-phone to someone in this area code but was too short to complete the trace. The phone was found in your possession. The logical conclusion is that you were robbing a bank just eight minutes before a Greyhound bus headed for a cross-continental tour left the Boston terminal. Within those eight minutes you were being too closely tailed to have passed the loot to an accomplice in Boston. It is strange, however, that during final hours of your journey you didn't initiate even one call. But from the moment you disembarked from that bus, carrying a piece of luggage, you were being tailed till you dropped to the ground in the desert, where we picked you up, probably saving your life. Don't you think you owe us one?"

"I've never been so blatantly accused of having performed a felony," I replied, infuriated at such a suggestion. Robbing a bank? And yet the bank I entrust with my finances! But now you have me thinking about what might have happened."

I'm sorry, but all the evidence points in one direction Mike. You are the only one we find that fits the circumstances. The time you bolted from your city, Boston; the proximity of the robbed bank to the bus terminal; the time of the robbery; the short phone call coming from your cell phone; the proximity of the receiver of that call to the locale where you alighted from the bus; the phone being found in your possession; there's too much evidence against you to just wish it away. Unless you can disprove any part of the evidence I'm afraid you're the culprit.

Carefully trying to recall everything that happened during those past couple of days, I began to appreciate how important each minute event could be, in order to save my skin. Controlling my rage, I casually asked, "Hugh, can I have a blank sheet and a pencil? Thanks. Now please call out each one of those silly names you were able to dig out of that SIM card, and carefully spell each one of them."

"Sure, if you think that will help solve the problem. Barum Darum, Blewbury Pi, Flufy Flour, Mugsy Bugzy, Mumbles Bug, Riski Wiski , . ."

"Did you spell that with four "I's" or are there any "Y's"?" "All are with four "I's". After that we have Rodum Dodum . . ."

"Okay Hugh, I think that's enough. I think I understand what all that means. Every group of two words consists of ten letters.

"Hugh took a moment to examine the rest of the list and said, "Yes. There are ten letters in every group. So what does that prove?"

Each letter represents a digit on the phone pad, right?"

"Each one of those name groups is a telephone number. They show the area code and seven more numbers. In order to completely decipher them all, would take some time, but we can assume that they are phone numbers."

"So what does that mean to us? If we don't have precise phone numbers, how can we phone any of them?" Asked Hugh, who might have been successful in browbeating suspects, but his sense of deduction proved to be much slower than his physical bulk.

"Why would you want to call all of them, or even any of them? They aren't the robber. They're his contacts.

It then struck me, what most probably happened. Since my dear mother's phone number was not registered in the SIM card in our possession, my phone must have inadvertently been exchanged with that of my seatmate on that bus.

"Hugh, I'm beginning to remember a few things about the time I got onto the bus in Boston. I found a seat about half way back on the right hand side. It was an unoccupied double seat and I slid over to the window side. A plain looking man, probably in his thirty's was the last one on the vehicle. He had arrived with a large duffle bag that he refused to have checked into the baggage compartment, and was perspiring profusely when he clambered up the steps of the bus, just as the driver was getting prepared to get moving on his scheduled run. Seeing that he wouldn't be taking on any more passengers, he didn't make an issue about the duffle bag being in the aisle beside this last passenger to arrive. Physically, he was comparable to me hence those who sought him erroneously trailed me from the moment I alighted from the bus in Blink, Nevada, where I left the bus, but he remained to continue his trip.

"If I have his cell-phone he must have mine. And if he is using it to dial outgoing calls, probable suspects that his coded name list became corrupted, as much digital data is apt to. He might not suspect that he isn't using his own phone, even though he isn't receiving calls. Should I take a chance and call my own number offering to re-exchange our phones?"

Hugh's face cracked open with a big smile. Hey! That's great thinking. Just wait till I tell Jake and Willie they were following the wrong man all along."

"**H**ugh," I sobered him up a bit. "They wouldn't like being told that they lost their man while following a red herring. We have to plan a positive approach."

"**S**o what do you suggest?" He asked. With that, he now put me in charge of suggesting the strategy.

"**B**efore I go into that I'd like to know with whom I'm working. You guys could just be a gang of crooks who want to use my brains so you can get your hands on the loot for yourselves.

"**O**h! You are some smart cookie. Yah. I guess you have a right to be suspicious. Just a moment and I'll get my mates," and called out, "Jake. Willie. Come on in and join us here." Within a moment we were joined by Hugh's coconspirators, who had been following our conversation all along, so it wasn't necessary to repeat anything. Hugh then added, "Okay guys, shall we identify ourselves to Mike? After all he is still holding a winning card. And without it we still have a long way to go till we catch up with our prey and he has a full day's head start on us."

After mulling over the suggestion, Jake said, "I guess we have little to lose by that. And if Mike is just playing for time we still have him in custody. Haven't we? So go ahead and show him your ID."

Hugh reached into his shirt pocket and produced a small wallet, that when flipped open displayed his FBI badge. After I took that in, the other two did the same.

"**W**ell Mike?" asked Hugh. What plan do you have up your sleeve? How do we catch up with the robber?

"**W**hat do you say, I phone up my own phone number. As soon as he hears the jingle, that's probably a lot different from the one he's used to, he may be suspicious and may not answer my call. And if I call again and a third time, he might become curious and receive the incoming call. I can try to keep him on the "line" for a couple of minutes discussing our trip as seat-mates and the fact that he's using my phone while I have his. I'll try to convince him that we should return each other's phone, because he probably has contacts that he wishes to keep track of.

"**A**ll this time you guys will be in contact with the service provider tracking the receiving end of the call by whatever means they can. Triangulation, by location and distances between their relay antennae, or any other system they employ. In that way you'll be able to find your fugitive as well as the cash, I'll get my phone back and I can get back to work.

"However before we can continue I need some pure water to wash down that mud you guys gave me for breakfast?"

"Sure!" Said Hugh, with a grin. "It was great to see you getting all chocked up over such a meal. Myself, I would never become so emotional over a cup of cocoa."

I took a long drink then added somewhat facetiously, "Thank you."
"Okay. Here goes. And I punched in the phone number to my cell-phone. After a heart-stopping delay of probably no more than three seconds, listening to the beeps verifying that the ring-tone of my phone was playing its melody before receipt of the call was confirmed, when our prey pushed the left hand top button on the phone pad that was in his possession. He was slow to open the dialogue, probably harboring some suspicion at the melody being so different from the one he was so used to. So I opened with, "Hello! Hello!"

"Yah," was his opening, and only word.

I continued, "Hi. I believe we know each other. We shared the same bench on the bus from Boston for a couple of days."

"Yah. Could be. What do you want?"

"First of all I wish to apologize for ignoring your presence during that long trip. We hardly had a word between us during all that time."

"That's okay. I had something on my mind too, and didn't feel like talking anyway. So why are you calling now? And how did you get my phone number? You don't even know my name"

I continued with a slow drawl in order to stretch out the conversation as best as I could to buy more time. "Well my name is Mike, in case I didn't tell you while we were traveling together. What's your handle?"

"Yah. Well I'm called Butch by my best friends. But how did you know my phone number?"

"Well Butch, that's what I wanted to tell you."

Jake, wearing a set of headphones nodded animatedly towards me and held up his left hand with his thumb and index finger forming an "O", indicating that he was progressing with the track. His right hand gripping a pen, was busily scribbling some figures on a sheet of paper.

"Yah. Well what was that?"

"Butch, I got through to you because you have my cell phone. And I think that I have yours. I probably picked yours up off the seat by mistake when I left the bus, and forgot mine on the bus. So you must have picked it up from the seat afterwards. The one that you're now holding is mine. That's how I was able to contact you. I called my own phone."

"Oh? Yah. Could be. Since you got off the bus I only got a couple of wrong numbers from some old lady. So the couple of calls I made on yours will be on your bill. Haw Haw. But that's not so much. Maybe it'll cost you a couple of bucks, but not more than ten. That's the price you pay for losing your phone. Haw Haw."

I guess that put him into a mellower mood, so I was able to suggest . . .

"Butch what do say we switch back our phones? You probably have all your girls' phone numbers on it. Are you far from Blink, Nevada, that little town where I left the bus? I can be there in a bit over an hour, and we can meet at the bus stop there. Is that okay with you?"

When a few seconds passed in total silence, I began to panic. Was he suspicious and about to disagree? But he came on once more, "Okay. But it'll take me about three hours to get there. The bus around here doesn't run every ten minutes like in a big city"

The plan worked to perfection. The FBI got their man. The bank got all their money back and because I, as a loyal citizen who helped put the FBI on the right track was promised a reward from the bank for my cooperation with the authorities.

My mother had been silently listening to the entire story but still didn't appreciate why I hadn't acknowledged her repeated calls properly. Instead she admonished me, "My dear Mike, see what your meddling with filthy sewage has gotten you into? Having to associate with such crude characters? I always told you, you'd have met a nice girl; if you would have chosen to work at a clean job instead of meddling with those filthy cesspools that you seem to enjoy playing around with so much."

"Okay mom, maybe your right."

"What do you mean MAYbe!" Click. Tone . . .

THE FIRING SQUAD

Wow!!! What lines!! What exquisite contours! Who would have ever imagined? I've never yet seen such a superb model. But that's not all that prompted me to pursue the matter.

We'd been doing some impulsive traveling. Where we'd previously been really has no bearing on the matter. Right now we were searching for lodgings in London. Not having been aware of the situation, with big groups of tourists and professionals convening concurrently, every hotel we approached had no vacancy.

After hours of trudging through the city our teen-age daughter noticed a dreary looking building half-way down a side street that bore a sign "Hostelry." With a darkening sky as dusk was quickly falling, we concurred, "Anything would do, if they'd only have room for us."

The pleasant young clerk greeted us with, "You are in luck. We have one vacancy. Some bloke checked out just a few moments before you entered."

I thought to myself, "It must have been that elderly man with a small briefcase entering the taxi that had just sped off as we approached the hostelry."

Since we were a party of three he offered, "It might be a bit crowded, but I could arrange for an extra cot, of course, at a slight additional charge." The lobby seemed to be clean quite and well kept, but *any port in a storm* is way we felt after the many miles we'd been wandering around that afternoon.

The room, on the second landing was clean. Most important of all, we were not facing any gaudy signs that would be flashing all night, like we surely would have found had we taken a room in the middle of the entertainment district of the city.

As I usual do, I examined the furniture to decide how we'd organize our belongings for the next couple of days of our intended stay. When I opened the third drawer from the top of the dresser my eyes popped. There lay the most impressive camera I'd ever laid my eyes on.

Before realizing that it must have been forgotten by that old chap who so hurriedly checked out not more than a few minutes ago, I couldn't help but admire the complexity that went into creating such a masterpiece. It bore two turrets. One that held various lenses while the other one bore a selection of filters. With a flick of a wrist any combination of lenses and filters could be moved into position, and be ready for the perfect shot within a split second. The battery chamber was easily accessible and the mini-CD disk slot was rightly protected to prevent an accidental release If this was the professional photographer's dream, that old man must have been in an awful rush, to have abandoned such a treasure. It must have been a matter of life or death.

I charged down the stairs, not waiting for the unusually slow lift, as most hotel elevators tend to be, to reach the clerk at the front desk. "Sir," I called, "Have you any idea where that old man was headed for?" "Why? What's the matter? Is something wrong?"

"He forgot to take his camera. And it's a very special one too."

"I'm afraid he didn't leave any forwarding address; hadn't even given an address on his registration card at all. But he paid cash in advance for an entire week and left after only four days. "As he loped out like he was trying to escape from a charging rhinoceros he yelled, "Keep the change," jumped into the taxi that had been parked outside and they sped away. Had he asked me to order a cab, I would have some idea about how to track him down through the taxi company. But with more than three thousand legitimate companies it would be impossible to contact them all. I'm sorry I can't be of any help."

I couldn't shake the fact that someone, anyone, could possibly abandon such a unique camera.

Returning to the site of my discovery with my burning curiosity, that third dresser drawer still beckoned to me. I opened it still wider than I had the first time. There was a flier in the drawer, half in nd half out of a yellowing envelope. It was folded over and some of the text had been obliterated by gnawing insects over the years. When unfolded I found that most of the text was discernable.

FIRING SQUAD PARTICIPATION
To the personal attention of

Albert Dickson Ottawa, Canada

```
Date: 16th November 1947
Place: Green Bonnet Sports Arena
317 West Third, in the City of Pratt
This is the only notice you will be receiving
So follow instructions diligently
Appear promptly and in full dress.
Bring your own Colt 45 handgun


                    Nonattendance shall be
        PUNISHABLE by THE FULL EXTENT OF THE LAW.


Your presence is crucial to the success in the
pursuit of justice
Official order of
                            Your Commanding officer
                                Harry O'Henry
```

The title of such a weird document was quite shocking, even though it looked official and authentic. But my perusal of it was disturbed when I heard a bloodcurdling yell. My wife had just been doing a bit of exploring herself. I found her standing in front of the small refrigerator unit with the freezer door wide open. Facing her on the bottom shelf, covered with a coating of frost, but still quite discernable was a huge revolver. There were a few other suspicious items there too, but none of them were food stuffs.

After closing the freezer I tried soothing her down as she was well on her way towards total hysterics. I had her lie down on the bed, where fatigue caught up with her and she quickly fell asleep.

I'd never even imagined that such a document would ever be produced and distributed. Such a text was completely unbelievable. Could it have been a joke? And if so, it would be a very repulsive joke. But I read it with my own eyes.

At least I now had a name to attach to the stranger with a sixty-odd year old address, a quarter of the way around the world. Holding such a document in my hand and with the kind of items he had left in the freezer, worried me no end. Could he still be as dangerous as he might have been so very long ago? The pictures I envisioned were very mixed-up. His possessing such a dangerous looking weapon, owning such a beautiful camera, being in possession of such a damning piece of paper, and yet on the run. He's trying to escape from something or someone from his past. What goes on here?

After reading and rereading that notice my curiosity was piqued still further. I opened the freezer door once again and, with great trepidation, reached out for the frost-encrusted revolver that had lain there on the bottom shelf and removed it carefully. Walking over to the brighter table lamp I sought out any signs that would tell me if this was actually a Colt 45. After ascertaining that it certainly was, I quickly returned it to the freezer, hoping that my warm hands hadn't melted off enough of the frost for my finger-prints to transfer to this monstrous weapon.

My mind was working in overdrive trying to piece together all the odd things that had just come together and how they might amalgamate into a logical situation.

Had the old man once actually been part of a firing squad? Had he fired the blank? Had he actually shot and killed an unprotected individual at point blank range?

Oh! I did mention *firing the blank*, didn't I? Well some of you may not be aware of the fact, but it is usual for at least one member of a firing squad to have his gun armed with a *blank*, a bullet that is not capable of inflicting any damage. In that way no member of the squad is ever certain who actually fired the fatal bullet, and which one did not actually kill the victim.

Or had he been the target, and somehow escaped the punishment that he was to receive? And was he now tracking down those who had participated in that staged or organized murder of an innocent man? If so why did he leave without his weapon?

Or had he been a photographer who was supposed to record the event, and is now being hunted down by some party who wants information on other members of the squad? Might his hunter wish to destroy any evidence of that bizarre event? Might that possibly be his reason for the hasty escape? If that might be the case, are we, who are in possession of his camera and handgun not in mortal danger ourselves?

Or can this entire scene be a set-up to entrap us with all this deadly evidence in our hands? Why?

I hardly know what to think about the situation that puts my wife and daughter in danger. Where do I turn to for assurance or for assistance? Who can we trust who would not tie us up with the plot?

We just came to London for a bit of innocent tourism, to visit the museums that London is so famous for. We just wish to observe change of the guard at Buckingham Palace, to gaze at Big Ben when it strikes 12 at noon, to wander through the London Bridge museum, and to take in a night at the theater, no matter what was playing. Just to experience the thrill of it all.

Thank goodness our young daughter voted for a nap as soon as we entered the hotel room. All the wandering around for hours on end without a moment of rest was too much for her. By her being asleep she was completely oblivious of what had been going on during the past few minutes.

While my mind had been wandering through innumerable scenarios, subconsciously traversing so many mysterious computations, I hadn't realized that quite some time had past till both my wife Shirley and daughter Pearl had awoken almost simultaneously. Now that we were all awake I had to get my thoughts into a more positive level. It then dawned on me that we all must be quite hungry, not haven tasted anything since a light noontime snack. Maybe my mood would become more relaxed over a decent meal.

My suggestion that we go out to sample some food at one of the local restaurants was greeted enthusiastically. Without wasting any more time we descended to the lobby and asked the attendant if he could recommend a decent eatery in the vicinity.

"Well, if I may say so, Nothing in this neighborhood is really fit for touring folks like you are, but if I may suggest a really good Italian restaurant, that I'm sure you'll like, Tony and Rosa is the place for you. But it is a bit far, so you can pop into the cab that I notice standing just out front, and he'll have you there in a couple of minutes." Reading his name off the badge he was wearing on his left breast, I offered, "Thank you Roy. You sound so sure about Tony and Rosa, so we'll give it a try."

Sure enough there was a taxi waiting at the curb in front of the hotel, but just as we got there and he opened the doors for us, I excused myself and rushed back into the hotel, asking Roy for a visiting card so we'd know how to get back after the meal. "Good thinking! He replied. We lose a few clients once in awhile, when they leave the area and don't know how to get back here."

Armed with the address of our hostelry, I rushed back to the taxi, whose motor was already running. Shirley and Pearl were already seated in the back, while the vacant seat adjacent to the chauffer awaited placement of my posterior. I slammed the door shut, reached for the safety belt and we took off towards our destination. After some dozen blocks, traversing a couple of main arteries with a few zigzags we were duly deposited at the side entrance of Tony and Rosa's restaurant. Before leaving the cab I requested a visiting card so that we could contact the chauffer who knew his way around the city so well, paid the fare, and entered the so highly recommended eatery who's aromas were already enticing, even before being invited to be seated.

A menu was supplied to each of us bearing an explanation of authentic Italian restaurant terms with English translation for the various courses and a few important tips for the uninitiated:

For awhile the situation seemed to be too much for me to contend with, but after the three of us shared the **L'antipasto** I felt much calmer probably, due to the smooth sweet wine from a carafe that the waiter recommended

Interesting enough, none of us opted for any of the traditional Italian dishes one might expect. No pasta, nor any pizza.

A phone call to George brought our taxi to door within a short time. With less traffic on the roads the trip back to our hostelry was so much quicker than the original trip had been.

When we got back the night clerk on duty, who hadn't yet met us, handed over the key to our room with only a few of words, "The beds and the cot are made up and you now have fresh towels. Do you need a wake-up call?" I replied, "No, we'll be all right. Thank you. Good night."

I had hoped that I was right, but as soon as we entered the room, my mind began turning over all kinds of unconventional circumstances. The girls fell asleep very quickly, but I don't know how long I lay awake, till slumber overtook me. I was so overwrought that I didn't even remember if I had a nightmare or not.

The sun was quite high in the sky when I opened my eyes. I showered and dressed as quietly as possible. The girls still hadn't stirred. They must have really been tired; by the time they got into bed last night. But that's for the better. Who knows what today will bring, and how we might have to react to whatever might be in store for us? Better to be rested up as much as possible.

It was close to ten o'clock when Shirley stirred, glanced towards the wall clock, then jumped up into a sitting position, and asked, "How in the world did I sleep for so long? Could it be what we ate last night? Or might it be jet-lag catching up with me? Well, I don't remember ever feeling so rested as I do now. It could have been the wine. Could it be that powerful?

I guess the conversation, though subdued, was loud enough to arouse Pearl who turned and stretched while getting her bearings. We all finally got ourselves ready to go out for some breakfast. No matter how satiated we might have been from that late supper, hunger sets in long before ten hours have passed.

When they began unpacking and planning to arrange their stuff in the dresser drawers I calmly told them that the third drawer down is for my things, and not to disturb it. "I'll unpack my personal effects by myself."

Roy was back at the desk when we descended and on our way to the exit I asked if there was a decent eatery in the vicinity where we could have some breakfast. "Sure. Just on the corner with the next cross street there's a nice coffee shop."

So we headed in that direction, but not before noticing George sitting in his taxi right in front of the hotel, exactly where he had been parked last night. He seemed to be partial to this location.

Breakfast was quite filling, with fried eggs, warm well buttered buns and a fruit cocktail followed by coffee and a fresh cinnamon croissant.

Then back to the hotel to arrange our things and plan the rest of the day.

I managed to arrange my things so as to cover the camera from prying eyes and then spread out the few travel fliers that I'd picked up while in the lobby on the little table. After some study ad discussion we all agreed that we'd like to take in the British Museum and if time would allow, the Science Museum following a late lunch. That would delay the change of the guard till next day, due to the lack of time.

By nearly 11:00 o'clock we finally made our way out again, to be welcomed by George, who greeted us warmly, with both doors of his cab open. wide We had no other conveyance anyway, so accepted his jovial invitation, seated ourselves and as soon as he heard our plan sped off towards our destination.

Somewhere along the way I mentioned that he seems to favour the taxi stand, in front of that small hostelry. He replied "It's very convenient for me. I occupy the flat right next door." That seemed to make sense, and we continued our conversation about other sundry subjects concerning his interesting out-of-the-ordinary experiences as a cabbie in London.

When he dropped us off at the entrance of the British Museum we followed our preplanned tour of the cultural section of London, returning to the hotel quite late, but very much elated. Roy was still at his post and when we asked him to recommend a good restaurant, but something different from yesterday's, he asked if we'd ever tasted Jewish cuisine. I replied, "No, but am willing to give it a try." He gave us the address of a small not very sophisticated, but tasteful place, Moshe's Deli, a self-service restaurant.

After washing up from the day's exertions we made our exit. Sure enough George was ready to go and claimed to know the place. Actually it was not any further than Tony and Rosa's place had been but in a different direction, probably in the Jewish district of the city.

Here the atmosphere was somewhat brash and pleasantly lively. Many of the customers were choosing prepackaged portions of "take-out" packs for home consumption, but there were tables for those of us who chose to eat their interesting looking concoctions on the premises. We were warmly greeted and seated at a clean, cloth covered table. I rose from my seat and made my way to the long self-service table stationed under a banner that stated "No limit—all you want! You pay for a meal." The array was somewhat sorted into various categories; appetizers, soups, side dishes, main dishes, deserts, soft drinks, and hot drinks. Customers were approaching with empty plates and leaving with plates piled high with whatever they chose, returning to their tables to continue their meals.

It was with some effort, but we managed to eventually clear our plates. I promised myself that I must do it again sometime in the near future. Jewish cooking had such a mellowing effect on me that I completely forgot what was hidden back in our hotel room, and what consequences might they cause us.

Desert was out of the question. No way! Anyway it was long past the hour we should be getting into bed so I phoned George, who assured us that he would be there in a few minutes. We arrived at the hotel in record time to be greeted by the night clerk again that handed over the key to our room and returned to his studies.

As we were preparing for sleep my daughter asked me if I really paid attention to what George had said; when he told us that he favored the taxi stand in front of the hotel because he lived next door. I replied, "Yes, I remember. But why bring up the subject at all? And why right now?"

"Well, Dad, you were very intent on tracking down that old man who'd checked out of this room just before we moved in. Do you remember how you tried to get Roy to help you find the taxi that took him to whatever destination he was headed?" Beginning to get the drift of her message, I said, "Yes. It might very well have been George. He is our best possibility. Sure! He might remember that old man and to where he drove him. This was beginning to get my adrenaline pumping again but George must be tired after a full day on the road. I'll check with him first thing in the morning. Meanwhile we must get some rest and be prepared for a busy day tomorrow." With that, I didn't immediately fall asleep, but did, after awhile, from sheer fatigue.

I awoke early, showered, dressed and descended to the lobby, getting there just as Roy, the daytime clerk arrived. "Roy," I called out, "Do you remember when we had just arrived two nights ago, an old man had just checked out in a great hurry?" "Certainly, he was very generous with his tip as well. Is there still a problem with him?"

"Not really, but I'm surprised you didn't tell me about the taxi that usually parks out front, as probably being the one that he took to his destination. The chauffer told me that this is his usual taxi stand, and is there more often than any other cab. You should surely have known that."

"Actually that Tuesday was my first day on the job and I hardly knew about his habits. I'm sorry about that. But I sincerely hope that you were not put out by that fact."

My next step was to confront George himself, and hope his memory is as sharp as is his knowledge of London's roads. Descending the broad staircase to the sidewalkI made my way to the taxi that was already in position, with a smiling George already opening the passenger's door, with a cheery, "Top of the morning Sir. Where is the rest of the family?"

"Well George there's something I have to ask you. You may wish to decline giving me a reply, so I'll explain why it is imperative for me to know. Do you remember the old man that rushed into your taxi at dusk on Tuesday night?"

"I certainly do. But of what concern is it to you?"

"He forgot to take his very special camera along with him, and left it in the room we now occupy. I'd like nothing better than to return it to him. But I must discuss some very personal matter with him as well. Do you remember what his destination was?" "Of course I do. I've got a great memory."

"Could you drive me to that place?"

"Well it might not be entirely ethical, but I could deliver the camera and any note you might wish to send along. Then if he sees fit he could contact you."

"I don't think he'll know who I am, but the message that I have to give him requires a few questions and answers. It's a matter of life and death, and by now some lives have probably been lost."

"I'll have to think it over, Sir. Get back to me in about an hour. Okay?"

I felt that I was getting closer, but still had one barrier to overcome, and that was the human one. There is none more difficult to suppress that that of one guided by inflexible ethics. How much more must I divulge before I can convince George that the entire incident will not in any way confuse his personal conviction of what is correct behavior for someone in his position of trust.

I really didn't feel hungry, due to the anticipation of what might take place during the next few hours, but for the sake of the girls, I had little choice. I returned to our hotel room to find them all dressed and ready for breakfast. We went to same coffee shop where we had been on Wednesday morning, but having arrived at a much earlier time, found the place to be livelier. However we found the service was satisfactory, as well as the meal.

By the time we returned to the hotel a bit more than an hour had passed and it was time to contact George for his answer. Would our cabbie agree to take us on a ride to an unexpected adventure? I'd soon find out. I purposely called from our room so as not to be rejected face to face.

"Hello. George, this is Mr. Sandbar. Have you reached a decision about taking us out on the tour we discussed earlier?"

"I've given your proposal some deep thought and tend to believe your reason as being very serious. You don't seem to be a dangerous type, so would you be ready in about ten minutes? I'll fill the tank with petrol and check the oil just to be ready for highway travel. I'll meet you out front."

"I hurriedly removed the camera from its hiding place, carefully wrapping it up in a large bath-towel that I'd make sure to return and slipped the entire package into my traveling bag. With trepidation I slipped the printed document into its envelope, and put it into the inside breast pocket of my jacket, had the girls pay their respects to the rest room in anticipation of a long ride. On the way out I grabbed an empty envelope and slipped it into my pocket as well. Locking the door we made our way towards our rendezvous with George, who was just pulling into his regular parking spot. We took our regular places and set out for the unknown next step of our adventure.

Slough is a <u>borough</u> within the county of Royal <u>Berkshire</u>. The town straddles the A4 Bath Road (it becomes the Great West Road closer to London) and the <u>Great Western Main Line</u>, 22 miles (35 km) west of central London.

That is where we were headed, but with the elaborate preparations that George had made before making the trip, he had us imagining a trip of several hours. Of course getting out of London took more time than the actual highway trip took. A few blocks into Slough off the B416 highway brought us to the Pinewood Hotel. Now the problem was to find an elderly gentleman who at one time went by the name, Albert Dickson. I now realized that I should have attempted to find out if he was still going by that name, back at our London hotel. Before phoning Roy, though, I thought I would give it a try. Holding the empty envelope in my hand, with the incriminating one in my pocket, I approached the desk to inquire about a guest named Dickson. Sure enough he was registered under his own name.

With trepidation, I asked, "Would you please tell me what room Mr. Dickson is occupying? I have an urgent message to deliver to him personally?" The reply was of course, the expected, "I'm awfully sorry sir, but we cannot disclose such information. If you wish to have it deposited it with me, I'll make sure to notify him that he has a message in his mail box."

I was prepared for that kind of reaction to my request, so came back with, "I understand sir, but could you please let me know his phone extension so that I may speak to him?" With a smile, the desk clerk had an answer to that request as well. "I regret, very much sir but that would be divulging which room he is in, and it is against our policy to do so. I noticed that, as in most hotels, the array of little cubby-holes where the keys are usually kept, some of them contained envelopes, probably being held for pick-up by the lodgers. This gave me an idea. I jotted down my cell-phone number on the exterior of the blank envelope that I'd been holding all this time and asked for it to be placed in the mail-box of Mr. Dickson. "With pleasure, sir." And with that, he turned around and slipped it into cubby-hole number 218. So much for strict protection of the lodgers.

While the clerk was turned around with his back towards me I glanced at the top of a registration blank and memorized the hotel phone number, turned away towards the soft chairs placed in the lobby, where people usually meet others, pulling out my phone I dialed the hotel number, substituting the last three digits with 218. After a couple of ring tones the receiver on the other end was raised and following a few moments of apprehensive silence a shaky voice answered, "Yes? I received your message that I have a letter in my box, and was nearly out in the hall, on my way down. Is there something else?"

Now it was my turn to speak, and even though I'd rehearsed dozens of opening lines, I just said, "Albert, you don't have to run anymore. It won't be necessary for you to hide."

"Who is this? I don't understand what you're talking about. Hiding from what? From whom? Who are you, and why are you calling me?"

"Albert Dickson, your secret is not a private anymore. If you're willing to discuss the sixty year old matter I'll be very happy to return your camera to you personally."

"Who are you? What's your name? How do you know anything about me and what might have been my involvement in a sixty year old event? Why are you hounding me?"

"Relax Albert, you have nothing to fear. I know quite a bit about you and your buddies, but have no reason see any harm come your way."

"What is your reason for chasing after me in this way? What is your name anyway? You seem to know mine, so if you would be so good as to identify yourself, I might not be so apprehensive."

"My name is Pat Sandbar. Does that ring a bell?"

"What?? I can't believe you!! You're pulling my leg. How did you ever come up with such a name?"

"That's my name since birth. Surely you must know more about that name than I probably do. You were army buddies with my father and even served as best-man at his wedding. Albert. Are you still with me?" "Yes, I do know some of the history, but you're going to have to fill me in with more facts".

"You're crazy! Nobody knew about our deception, except for eight of us and the other seven are already dead. Where did you ever dream up such a concocted story?"

"Albert. It's time we met face to face and held a proper discussion. I know a bit but still have some questions that I must have answers to. Can we meet in your room? Or at any other place you choose?"

"Sure Pat, come on up to room number . . ."

"218. I know that already."

"Who told you that? Those desk clerks can't be trusted!"

"No it wasn't the clerk. I'm a professor of "Inferential Logics" on sabbatical leave from the University of Montreal, so it wasn't difficult to get such simple information as easily as I did. Just give me couple of minutes to get my wife and young daughter set up with coffee and cake, and then I'll be right up.

A knock on the door of 218 brought an immediate response, and the door swing open on silent hinges. Albert really looked aged, and I was surprised that at his age he could still be so agile, running from one hiding place to another. I was holding my traveling bag with the camera in my left hand so as to free up my right one for a hearty handshake. And Albert was no weakling!

"Come on over and sit down. What'll you have to drink?"

"Nothing strong, a cool drink would be welcome. Thanks."

"Now what is it you want to ask?"

Fishing the envelope containing the "firing squad" document out of my inner pocket, I slowly opened it, and with deliberate movements, removed the weird document. With even slower movements I unfolded it, turned it around and placed it on the table before Albert, who was meticulously following my every move. He glanced at it and closed his tired looking eyes for a few moments before reading it. His lips silently formed the words, letter by letter. I didn't disturb his slow progress through; it must have been at least two whole minutes for him to reach the end. He let out an audible sigh, leaned back in his easy chair and sat analyzing what he had read, probably trying to get his thoughts together.

"What can I tell you that you really wish to know about that occurrence?"

"Everything, it is imperative that I know everything that happened to cause such a terrible thing to happen. Should such an event have taken place during a war I would understand that some serious breach of security might have prompted such an act. But for such a punishment to be meted out to a soldier, two and a half years after the end of the Second World War doesn't make sense. You, Albert, having taken part in this operation, must surely be able to put some light on the matter. And don't tell me you can't remember details. And as the owner of such an exquisite camera you cannot tell me that there are such things as "minor" details."

"Where do I start?—We were a troop of nine soldiers responsible for the biggest warehouses receiving and distributing materials of all kinds, from thumb-tacks and staples to railway cars. The positions we held during and following the war demanded utmost trustworthiness, as we were responsible for billions of dollars worth of goods that were essential to the war effort. Everything had to be accurately accounted for and we did our utmost to fulfill our duty to the best of our ability.

However, our commanding officer, a scoundrel wearing the insignia of a major, his position went to his head. He organized the greatest wholesale black-market system imaginable. We ordinary members of the troop were supposed to cover-up for all the shortcomings and to falsify documents of incoming and outgoing materials.

With the end of the war, nearly all the troops were sent back to their countries of origin, but because our respective governments took it upon themselves to help with rehabilitation of war-torn lands with the materials that we would distribute to them, hence our mission continued to function unabated.

Our commanding officer, Major Harry O'Henry was so caught up in the system founded by him that it was virtually impossible to stop it. The Mafia and other organized criminal elements wouldn't sit by idly if their supplies were to be cut off. An attempt to reign in the volume of their supplies brought more pressure on him. Much more than might have been from the government institutions that were sending shiploads of commodities to our warehouses on a daily basis. Threats to his life were commonplace.

He then thought of a plan to free himself, from both the legitimate sources and his illegitimate clients. He would set up an official court-martial finding an innocent member of his troop guilty of all counts; stealing from public stores and black marketing, leaving him holding the bag. Through his elimination by a "firing squad" he would clear himself then arrange for a quick escape back to his country of origin with a clear slate. Any and all shortcomings would be buried along with his scapegoat. He had a brilliant plan, but we couldn't allow one of our innocent buddies be set up as a sacrifice for such a guilty bastard.

He began preparing his plan and even went as far as registering the punishment with the Canadian Army Headquarters, receiving permission to follow through with his *scheduled performance.*

As in any "firing squad" the weapon of at least one member of the troop is loaded with blanks. In effect no one knows which one that is so that in that way each one can feel psychologically, that he is not the one who fired the fatal bullet.

Not one of us, who knew of the goings on, wished to be an accessory to his macabre plan to murder one of our innocent buddies. We decided amongst ourselves that we would all load our pistols with blanks, except for one who would have live ammunition. He would not fire the first salvo. After firing blanks in Donald Sandbar's direction, we would all turn to put O" Henry in our sights and give him his rightful punishment, this time with all firearms.

It felt terrible to have to do such a thing, but he left us with little choice.

"How did you ever pull it off and get away with it? I would imagine that every man would have to be accounted for, even a dead soldier/"

That was the simplest thing. We switched dog-tags. Harry O" Henry was buried as the scoundrel who stole so many million dollars worth of public goods, but he was sent off carrying the ID of Donald Sandbar.

Our operation was duly closed down and we all returned to our respective homes. Several months passed and the entire incident calmed down, the real Donald Sandbar paid a condolence call to Harry's widow in Calgary. She had been notified that her husband went missing in action, but when she was told the facts about his disappearance, and knowing for sure that she was free of his attachment; she agreed to acquire a new identity and marry Donald, who might very well have been in a foreign military grave instead.

I was an avid photographer and agreed to be best-man on condition that they allow me to be their photographer at the wedding. Less than a year went by and you, Pat, were born.

"Shocking! But now so believable. I'm lucky to have found your camera, and appreciating its value, I was compelled to return it to you. Otherwise we might have never met. I still have two questions, though. What is the significance of that Colt 45 that you left in the freezer?"

"If you would have examined it closely you would have found that it has no firing pin. No matter how much I detest a man I would never be able shoot a man dead. What was your next question?"

"Why did you leave that hotel in London in such haste, even leaving your camera behind?"

"I really can't say. Somehow I felt that some ghost from the past was following me, and I couldn't get away quickly enough. But Pat, now that my eyesight is not so good, I want you to have the camera. The way you packed it and the care with which you handle it means you'll appreciate it.

COMMON SENSE ANNULS TESTIMONY OF TWO VALID WITNESSES

When all three surveyed the hall from behind their dais, from whence they were supposed to be in total control of the proceedings, they didn't find the scene amusing. A young woman sat on the plain wooden unpadded chair, behind an old oblong bare table. It had stood in this very same place for as long as anybody could remember. Even a simple tablecloth might have covered all the scratches and other mutilations that had defaced its surface by countless previous occupants of this same chair, probably due to their nervous reactions, of just having had to sit in that seat. But even a simple table covering was not part of the array, and only added to the dismal scene.

Her tears had already ceased to flow, but the mess they made of her makeup left their mark, even her tinted glasses could not conceal. Her well dressed toddlers, dolled up in neat, though not new, clothing were still quite clean even though the two of them were frolicking around on the hard seats, on either side of their mother. Their restlessness was probably due to, either boredom, or because the straight-backed wooden chairs made it uncomfortable for them to sit still.

A small plain table and simple padded chair was in place, to the right of the dais, whereupon sat the court stenographer. His fountain pen poised in his right hand that when pressed into service would continue writing upon folio sized lined pages with blue ink. His task was to record in full, every word uttered in connection with the proceedings of the case. From the growing stack of pages on his left, it was quite obvious that much had already been recorded since the opening of this session.

A couple of slowly revolving ceiling fans that were supposed to keep the air moving couldn't even build up enough of a breeze to ruffle the pages on the stenographer's desk.

To the left of the judicial trio stood the traditional witness stand, as it is usually referred to, raised up off the level of the floor and accessed by ascending two well worn wooden stairs, and presently, the second witness of the day's proceedings occupied the comfortably upholstered seat. However he didn't really look very relaxed there, as he was being gently admonished by one member of the board of judges.

Behind the young lady several rows of plain wooden chairs were arranged, with an aisle between the right and left sections. These seats were made available to accommodate any spectators, who might wish to observe court proceedings. On this particular day the audience was made up of only four persons, one of which was a very young lad, nominally I, who accompanied my grandfather on his many searches for interesting places to visit in the city. He was perfectly correct in his belief that such experiences would aid me in forming a wide range of knowledge and build up character towards later years in life. Heaven bless his memory!

The three justices sat comfortably behind the dais upon well padded chairs, upholstered with shiny soft black leather. Their seats were built to swivel either which way, adding to their utmost comfort. The adjudicator on the left addressed the perspiring witness, who was quite ordinary; not young, nor aged, yet not really middle-aged either. He had obviously not shaved for at least two weeks. He wore not new but well taken care of clothing, his shoes probably never having been caressed by a brush since the day he acquired them, and neither had his hair been combed since his last haircut, probably at least two months or more ago. But he looked quite dapper, despite his lack of personal grooming.

"Young man," exclaimed the judge, "I herby repeat myself once again, hoping that you understand my simple instructions. Please tell the court how you came to be in the house on Doshon Road where the tragedy occurred while you were there. Please tell us in the singular about yourself, and don't tell us about 'us' or 'we'. Tell us only about you yourself. Do you understand?"

"**Y**es sir, your honor. I'll try to get it right this time. I was walking by foot on Doshon Road in the direction of the traffic circle leading into town. Just as I was passing the little wooden house, the place where the terrible tragedy happened I felt an odd change in the weather. A very strong wind suddenly came up. I was afraid that the way it was building up into some kind of storm, changing direction with every moment that passed that I might be blown off my feet. When tried to change my direction and head for the little house to seek shelter there, the wind became so ferocious that I was sure I was being caught up in a tornado. It took a lot of effort for me to finally reach the entrance where I banged on the door several times. Oh! Just the thought of it makes me cringe! That horrendous place, now no more than a pile of charred rubble, and a horrible memory gives me the shivers."

The judge interrupted with, "I understand the turmoil that you are experiencing, but please stick to the facts, and try to control your emotions. You may proceed now. Thank you."

The witness shook his head quickly, from side to side, continuing with his narrative, "My heart felt heavy when I realized that there no answer to my heavy knocking on the door. Suddenly the shadow of another man came up beside me. He tried to tell me something but the shrieking wind overpowered his voice. When I turned to look at him I made out that he was trying to tell me that even if anybody was at home nobody would hear our banging on the door and frenzied call for help over the noise of the wind. He was probably just as worried about getting some kind of shelter from the constantly strengthening storm that was building up without mercy as I was. I grasped the door knob with my hand and through a normal tendency to turn a knob, the door was flung open from the force of the wind and I was literally pushed into the house, falling on the floor. The other person who had been crouched behind me was thrust through the doorway and fell upon me, where we both lay for a moment, entangled one with the other. With utmost exertion, it took the combined effort of the two of us, to swing the door back into place far enough to engage the lock latch into the strike hole. I don't know about the other guy but I was hoping that the house would stand up to the battering of the steadily increasing acceleration of the wind.

It was getting to be gloomy so I searched around for a light switch, found one but the bare bulb that was swinging from a thin wire from the middle of the ceiling didn't go on. I thought that there might be a power failure but noticed that a kerosene lantern was hanging on the wall. I don't carry matches, but my new-found buddy extracted a lighter from his pants pocket and together we got the wick burning, and the glass chimney in place, replacing the lantern to its nail. At least we'd have some light o keep us company, as the gathering storm was dimming the daylight very quickly.

Just as we completed this task, we heard some heavy thumping on the door. Glancing at each other we realized that some other human being was trying to find shelter from what had become an unbelievable tempest. Well lucky for him that we could help save him, so we both jumped to the task of opening the door against the pressure of the wind, enough to allow our guest to enter the house we had sequestered for the duration of the storm.

Our guest made it into the house but the battle that he had been waging till he got to the house just about finished him, and when he saw a bedroom straight ahead, wobbled his way directly to the bed and was probably asleep long before he hit the pillow. We were now three refugees from the storm in a little wooden house.

The house was not big at all; we really didn't have a chance to examine the rest of it. We knew that there was an entrance/living room and a bedroom. There must have been a kitchen. After all it is a house, and every house has a bathroom as well. But before we could actually wander through the house to check things out, it struck!

Duties of the court warden, stationed just to the right of the pair of double entrance doors, though presently quite idle, were at times challenging to his multi-tasking abilities. He was responsible for the order and decorum of the courtroom. His was the job to monitor each and every person and whatever items they might be bringing along, before allowing them entrance into the vaulted square hall. He was to enforce the rule that no food or beverages were carried into the chamber. Of course in this case, a couple of baby bottles were allowed entry as an exception, in order to control the two small children who were in attendance with their mother. The warden also was responsible to assure that witnesses, who had been examined, had no opportunity to discuss their testimony with those who had not yet been questioned. In general, he had to keep a sharp eye for whatever might cause a disturbance to the proceedings.

"Just having had a chance to quickly size up the house, I saw that it had not been modernized very much. A wood-burning stove stood on a square of concrete in the living room facing the bed room, separated from the wooden wall by a sheet of asbestos as insulation. A blackened iron stovepipe from the stove went through the roof, to direct smoke out of the house when in use. I had hardly had a chance to turn toward, what I had surmised to be the kitchen when a lightening bolt struck the metal chimney and came through to the old iron stove simultaneous with an accompanying crash of the thunder. I had never before experienced such dread as the entire structure violently shook. The kerosene lantern was loosed from its nail on the wall and as it hit the wooden floor burning fuel spread out literally sealing us off from the bedroom, where this stranger was fast asleep. There was no way we could have got trough the scorching flames to try and save him from the escalating inferno, as the flames spread ever so quickly consuming the dry wood floor as if a river had broke its dam.

We, the two of us, managed to barely escape through the entrance door and run towards the rear of the house to see if we could, in some manner or another, rescue the stranger. However . . .

The square structure was built on a very steep terrain. Even though the front of the house was level with the earth, the rear was supported on four wooden columns, and the floor was at least two meters from ground level at this point. The window was still higher that that from the ground. Steel window bars had been installed, to keep out intruders making it impossible for him to have escaped by that way. There was no way we could conceivably get to our friend, nor was there any door at the rear through which he might escape, even had he been awake and coherent at the time this catastrophe was developing with such momentum.

It probably took, not more than five or six minutes, before the entire structure was a smoldering pile of rubble, with only a few steel pipes, part of the plumbing system sticking up out of the ruins. May his soul rest in peace!"

A pathetic sob escaped from the poor widow's lips, deeply grieving for her husband who had most certainly been reduced to ashes.

"**B**lessed is the true judge!" escaped the mouth of the court stenographer, whose emotions were instinctively stirred by the witness's recollections of that fateful event.

Deliberation was delayed no further, and within moments, all three judges had unanimously concurred that the stranger was indeed dead, and the widow would be free to remarry if and when she would deem it proper to do so.

The moderating judge who had occupied the central position slowly entwined the fingers of his left hand with those of his right hand and closed his eyes, while slowly considering how to organize his words. His deliberation extended for somewhat more than a minute. He then opened his eyes and tenderly directed his declaration towards the young woman, and pronounced: "In accord with, and based upon the testimony of two dependable witnesses and in order to avoid any further grief to this woman and to her family, this court unanimously declares her husband is hereby officially declared—

At this juncture, and before the court warden realized what was taking place the pair of doors swung open into the hushed courtroom and a disheveled unshaven man burst in and continued striding towards the dais, bellowing, "NO! Stop the proceedings!"

The entire court was shrouded in shocked silence, as twelve pairs of eyes swung around to face the man, and every last one of them remained speechless for a moment, before utterances of surprise broke up the unobtrusively heavy silence with voices shouting from every direction. The two children had already sprung off their seats and rushed to their father, each hugging a leg of his badly ripped and filthy pants. Their screams were squeals of glee, while most others were cries of surprise of disbelief as this hearing was taking a new tack. His wife was so emotionally overcome that she was about to fall into a swoon, and just about fell into the arms of one of the spectators, who sensed what was happening. The court warden finally got to his feet and rushed after the intruder, but was so overcome by surprise that when the newcomer suddenly stopped at a distance from the judge's dais, he collided with the uninvited trespasser sending them both sprawling on the surface of the well waxed wooden floor. As they were becoming untangled from one another, the moderator had already grabbed up his gavel and while hammering furiously on the dais, yelling, "Order in this court! Order in this court!" This continued for some time, till a semblance of silence was restored. He then inquired of the interloper, "May we be apprised regarding your impudent entrance into this court of law? Baring a very valid reason I could have you held in contempt of court, so please be careful how you address this court."

"I'm sorry, your honor. But please understand that I am the very same person you were about to officially declare dead." He raised his arm and spaced his thumb and forefinger to less than a millimeter between them, and continued. "You were this far from authoritatively declaring my dear wife a widow, and my lovely children as orphans. I had little choice, but to make as fast an entry as possible to prevent that. Requesting a formal audience would have been too late. Now is it too presumptuous of me to ask for a drink of water. I haven't had a sip in over two days."

"Warden! Please give this man some water. We have a lot to discuss with him at this time, and I wouldn't want his to pass out in this court," requested the judge, and his instructions were immediately followed.

"Now, sir, would you please take the stand and tell us how you come to be in this court, when it was believed that you were burned to death in a conflagration that took place two days ago. If you were saved from the burning building, why didn't you show up earlier? This is a serious situation and we are in no rush, so take your time." He addressed the court, and asked, "Your honor, if I could be spared the anguish of sitting in a witness box I think my mind would work better, so with the court's permission, may I sit in a regular chair?"

The judge acquiesced to his request, and after choosing a seat beside his wife, began his narrative. "A tremendous noise woke me up from a deep sleep. As far as I know I was all alone in a strange bed in a room that I didn't recognize, and the whole building was shuddering. In front of me, I saw a thick wall of fire reaching upwards from the floor and curling onto the ceiling. The popping sound of burning wood convinced me that something dynamic was happening, and if I was to save myself I would have to think fast. I couldn't remember how I ever got to be there, but I had to escape, and very quickly. When I turned around I observed that a window covered by steel bars blocked that possibility of any exit. The room was quickly filling up with smoke, but I noticed a narrow door in the far left corner of the room and with a couple of strides, was able to open it. Hoping that it would lead to the outside, but to my horror, I found myself trapped in the confines of a shower cubicle. Actually this, in a way, is what saved my life.

The first thing I did was to turn on the shower. Immediately, becoming totally drenched, as cold water cascaded upon me, though fully clothed, it was a good way to keep the air from becoming smoky. Another glance around me and I noticed that an additional shower head hung on a hook. This one was attached to a flexible hose with a trigger to control the flow of water. I tried it out on the door that was becoming hotter each moment, and found that when I spayed cold water on its surface I cooled off considerable. At least the fire could be temporarily held at bay if I could prevent the wooden door from burning. And that's what I did. For how long? I have no idea if it was for ten minutes, twenty, or even longer. It felt like there would be no end to my ordeal with the blaze virtually surrounding my little cubicle.

Not realizing how tiny this shower stall was, I had been standing on the drainage hole, preventing water from leaving and the surface of the water rose with each moment till I was more than chest high in the deepening confined chamber. This caused me to consider the possibility of a new problem. I still hadn't understood that it my own foot that prevented the water from draining. Was I saving myself from burning, to die by drowning? What a horrible choice to make!

Then my lucky break came as unexpectedly and as suddenly as one may imagine. Unbelievable but miraculously, the weight of all that water along with me on that floor, was resting on a large wooden beam that ran under the floor from the front of the house to its rear right under the shower stall. For some reason that is only known to the One in heaven, the front end of the beam burned through and disconnected itself from the shell of the structure, allowing it to slip away, and releasing the floor of shower stall from its mooring. As I fell through the hole where till then, a floor had been supporting me, I still had a grip on the flexible hose, thereby finding myself hanging by one arm in space, under the blazing building, probably a meter above the ground. As soon as I realized what my position was, and seeing the entire floor and its understructure a burning inferno, I released my grip on the hose, tumbling to the ground. Due to the steep pitch of the ground level, I rolled down the incline, quite way till I was caught in the underbrush of a thicket. There I was stopped and must have dozed off.

I had no idea how long I'd been asleep, but when I awoke I was very thirsty. I made my way up the sheer slippery incline, passing a pile of charred wood and ashes. The only things standing up were a few steel pipes and an old iron stove.

I finally got to Doshon Road and headed into town. At the traffic circle I turned left into the city, looking for a place where I could wet my lips. All thoughts of finding a drink left me as soon as I noticed a headline in the morning newspaper, "Local Tribunal to Hold Hearing about Missing Person in Doshon Road Fire." "Fear that he was totally consumed in the fire, his surviving wife will probably legitimately be declared a widow, etc."

As soon as I saw such news, all else escaped my mind till I hurried over to this court in order to prevent a tragedy from taking place.

Utter silence filled the court room as the new evidence was being comprehended. Not a sound escaped the lips of anyone in the entire chamber, till . . .

One of the spectators, an unknown stranger, who sat throughout the entire case without uttering a word, but he'd apparently been paying attention to the entire proceedings, raised his right hand and requested permission to address the court. Permission was duly granted. He rose up to stand on his feet, and from the spectator's section facing the dais, began, "The Torah states, in rough translation, *'On the verbal testimony of two or three witnesses shall he, who is to be put to death, shall die, but on the verbal testimony of one witness, he shall not die.'* How are to understand the meaning of *he, who is to be put to death, shall die?*

We find that the Torah stresses that valid testimony is only accepted from two or three reliable witnesses; however this statute can be nullified by common sense. Such a case has just now taken place before our very eyes, when the one who was about to be declared deceased actually showed up very much alive, annulling the testimony of two reliable witnesses. Their testimony had nearly succeeded in having him declared dead, but he showed up to prove that a live person cannot be presumably confirmed as dead, even if his testimony is by the mouth of a single witness. So, young man, as long as you were alive you really had nothing to worry about, regarding the presumption that you were legally dead. Go ahead and keep on living.

The presiding judge was amazed at the simple commentary of such a complex Torah statement. Addressing the distinguished gentlemen, he exclaimed, "What genius! You, sir, should be sitting here behind the bench." To which, with a twinkle in his eye, the visitor replied, "Thank you, your honor. But I've already retired from that position.

Nearly speechless, the judge could barely declared, "Court Adjourned!"

GILL BONDS & DILL DISSOLVES

Rabbi Gill's brother, Dill is a much sought after divorce lawyer.

Al who had spent much time behind "iron" bars asks the lawyer if he can have his brother, Rabbi Gill explore his chances of a successful marriage with his fiancée.

Dill warns Al that since he's not Jewish his brother cannot marry them, but he'll try and convince him to test their compatibility as a successful match.

After having attentively listened to Rabbi Gill Oberman's non-proselysive introductory guide to Judaism, Allen and Ellen entreat the Rabbi to convert them.

Rabbi Gill attempts to dissuade them with his reply, "That's another story".

This narrative is entirely a factionary account of a possible situation. Any such characters are only an abstract idea that has been forming in my mind for some time and has no bearing on reality.

I'm sorry sir; but can you please just move over for a moment?

Without even bothering to turn his head to face Dill he grunts? What's bothering you?

You're leaning on the mail slot and I have to deposit a letter.

Why don't you use Email? Or a Blackberry? That way nobody's going to tamper with your mail.

Dill patiently replies, nobody ever tampers with my mail!

How can you be so sure? If you don't receive a letter once in awhile how do you know it hasn't been tampered with?

That just doesn't happen. I get all my mail, and if I don't get it—it hasn't been sent out. Hey! I know you from somewhere.

Sorry to disappoint you, but the only way you'd know me, is if you spent a good part of your life behind bars.

Well, as a matter of fact, I did pump beer at Dinty Moor's on Second Avenue for a couple of years. That was how I paid my way through college.

So you're the guy who had me sent up for two years.

No! That was probably my brother Gill. He's the respectable one in the family. He couldn't see anything funny about an attempted robbery so he pushed the silent alarm and kept your attention while trying to dissuade your attempt. You have only yourself to blame for continuing the conversation till the cops showed up.

Tell me about your brother, the super honest one. How does he make a living if he's so scrupulous?

By the way what is your name? Here we are chatting all this time and we haven't even introduced ourselves.

Uh! Okay. You can call me Al. What's yours?

That's all right Al, I should have introduced myself first. My name is Dill, and I make my living entirely different to that of my brother Rabbi Gill. I became a barrister after leaving Dinty Moor's where I served behind the bar till I passed my final bar exams. That's when. I passed the job on to my brother Gill who was then studying for the Rabbinate. Now that he's a practicing Rabbi, one of his favorite functions is officiating at weddings.

Does he call a cop if he doesn't like the looks of the bride or the groom?

Oh no! Gill would never do such a thing. Before he agrees to officiate he interviews the couple, each one separately and then together to observe their attitude and how they respond to each other when he brings up some provocative subject or other. He carefully chooses a topic that should cause some fractious reaction between the love-birds and judiciously observes how they discuss, debate or argue about it.

This litmus test is repeated several times before he agrees to wed them. Actually he is more of a physiatrist than a run-of-the mill matchmaker. When he performs a wedding ceremony the marriage is an everlasting one. That of course, is why he's so successful at his calling and the couple is usually more than happy to pay the fee that they themselves decide upon. Rabbi Gill has earned an exceptional status, especially in that field.

That's enough for him to make a decent living? Performing a wedding every once in awhile?

I don't think you understand. His reputation is immaculate and demand for his service is without a doubt, constant.

You seem to be so proud of your brother. What's your profession?

I'm a divorce lawyer.

Oh! That's great. What a racket! So you're a barrister, still behind bars, while I'm out free already. He—He. That's really funny. Tell me, how many of your brother's patrons end up in your office? I like that. Gill hitches them up and you unhitch them.

Actually you're going to be surprised when I tell you that I've never been approached by even one couple who's been married by my brother. He's very careful about allowing an obvious mismatch to pass his compatibility assessment of the pair.

Now, you tell me. Is that proper compensation? You got him a job when he needed it and now he won't even put any business your way. What kind of family do you belong to anyway?

My older sister Mina is a marriage councilor who runs a very successful business. She never mentioned, during or many conversations, that any of her clients were among those married by our brother, Rabbi Gill. But has plenty of work with incompatible couples who opted for marriage ceremonies by other Rabbis. And some of them, though she never identifies them, they are so far from ideal marriages that for most of the time she spends with them she's preventing one or the other from strangling his or her partner, right there in her office. How they ever even thought they could live together to begin with is entirely incomprehensible.

She has had some success stories in her career, but some are downright silly disagreements that have no real basis to them.

For instance there was the couple who wanted to separate due to a roll of toilet paper.

Toilet paper? What could a roll of toilet paper have to do with incompatibility in a marriage?

You'll laugh when I tell you, but this was a serious fixation with them. She wanted the roll to hang with the tail against the wall and he insisted that the tail hang away from the wall.

And that was a sufficient disagreement to warrant seeing a marriage councilor?

You bet it was, and they were even willing to pay her mediation fee.

So did they separate, and approach you for a divorce on that silly dispute?

No, I never got to meet them. My sister came up with a simple but brilliant solution to their problem. She suggested they install an adjacent toilet paper holder so that one held a roll with its tail against the wall and the other one held a roll with its tail away from the wall. However, not many solutions were as simple to solve as that one,

Hey! She's pretty smart, your sister Mina. See? I'm getting to know your family already. Not bad for an uneducated ex-con, even if I have to say so myself. Have you got any other stories to tell about her job?

Well there was one couple who complained that the wife wasn't preparing their food to her husband's liking. In every cake that she baked, she'd add chopped nuts, and he was very much allergic to nuts. She claimed that she loved nuts in her cake, and if he didn't like it he could buy himself cake without nuts. But she wasn't going to suffer just because he couldn't eat nuts. He could buy any kind of cake he wished but she wasn't going to change her recipes just for him. He had one other choice. He could serve her with divorce papers.

What a stupid reason to seek a divorce. Unless she just wanted to get rid of him.

Except that she swore up and down that she loved him very much and was just being stubborn about her expertise in the kitchen. She just didn't wish to mess up her recipes for, what she termed, his whims.

So how did she save this marriage?

It took a lot of convincing, but eventually Mrs. agreed to pour part of the cake mixture into a separate baking tin before adding the nuts to the remaining portion for a separate cake to her own liking. She was afraid that that simple act would spoil her recipe but was surprised when it even improved her smaller cake.

Then there's the couple that sought her services because the husband insisted that his wife iron every piece of his clothing, including his underwear, socks and even his bath towel. Naturally she refused, claiming that it was a stupid demand of her, especially with her household workload, and caring for their newborn twins.

That sounds quite inane, but how did she advise them on that one?

I don't remember, but they finally came up with a compromise. I do recall, however that Tina was called in on that one.

That's the social worker. Right?

You bet. And she's a great one at that.

This Mina seems to have a lot of interesting cases.

Here's another one that was even more complex. The couple wouldn't even show up together. When both finally took their seats, they made sure to sit quite distant one from another. The atmosphere was heavy with loathing.

What was their problem?

It started with garbage. He was supposed to take out the garbage every morning on his way to work.

Isn't that usual? Every man of the house removes the garbage.

Yes. But his complaint was that she purposely wraps up the garbage in such a way that half way down the stairs, the package bursts open and the rubbish fouls up the entire staircase. In his rush to work he hasn't got the time to scoop it up again so it remains there for her to clean up later on.

Right there and then she began yelling at him, (I'm leaving out the improper language that she peppered her harangue with,) "You purposely bust the bag of garbage and left it for me to clean up."

"So why didn't you wrap it up properly?"

"I always wrap it up as it should be. You just don't handle it properly, just to cause me anguish."

"Not so! I'd never do anything to hurt you like that."

"Oh no?" I can recite a whole list of the times you did senseless things just to spite me, just to hurt my feelings."

"That's not true. Besides, you hate my aunt Angela."

"How dare you accuse me of such a thing? What makes you even suspect such a thing?"

"You broke the beautiful cut glass fruit bowl she gave us as a wedding present."

"Well, it slipped out of my hands when I was washing it. That was not on purpose. Besides I really liked that bowl and used it often."

"You also detest my uncle Phil."

"How dare you make such a ridiculous accusation? I think very highly of him. I even call him "Uncle Phil" whenever he visits."

"Yes, you do. But only when he brings you flowers. But he when leaves you curse him up down the wall for leaving the toilet dirty after he uses it. He's not young any more and can't be expected to leave it spick and span when he finishes."

"And besides that you don't love me. I don't remember even one kind word from you, during the entire eight years we've been married. It's always complaints and criticism. You continuously spurn by attempts to show how much I care for you and love you. But I'm never good enough for you. You abhor all my relatives and never showed any kind of amity with any of them. You showed only animosity and denigration. Not a positive word about them from your lips. They've been so nice to us, yet you never showed reciprocal feeling towards them."

During all this time they were spitting venomous darts at each other. This was while they were in the presence of a stranger. Imagine how they related to each other in the privacy of their own home.

So how did your sister find a solution to this one?

She didn't. Once it came to insulting personalities she called in my younger sister Tina to consult on the case.

She found that the name-calling and cursing of relatives was too serious a situation for conciliation and after attempting to arbitrate between them, they came to one conclusion.

Eventually they were referred to me.

So you finally got your first case! Hey, good for you. How did you fare with them?

It was fortunate that even though they had been married for eight years there were no children to consider in the break-up. They were residing in a rented apartment and since she had no driver's license the car was no problem. Otherwise splitting up their meager belongings and bank balance was straightforward.

Strange as it seems, now that they're divorced they seem to be quite civil towards each other when they meet, even with their respective mates in tow.

Individually they are pleasant people but should never have been married to each other.

What about your younger sister, Tina. How does she fare?

She's a professional social worker, whose calling is quite broad. She may be called upon to deal with inter-related social problems at children's homes, religious institutions, medical clinics, clubs, community centers, courts, employment offices, family-aid bureaus, hospitals, schools, settlement houses and prisons. She must be prepared to advise and assist with craft and recreation services and youth services while dealing with delinquency problems.

Her activities are on a personal level with those who need her services. She doesn't work in an office. Its all house-calls, or wherever her help is required. Most of these cases are referrals from either a marriage councilor, the courts, medical institutions or where children may be involved, schools. Her workload is full and is often quite motivationally rewarding. It's in her personal nature to aid those who require help, even though many may not realize how much they would not cope without her being there when she is most needed. She has no fixed hours and has probably never enjoyed a prolonged vacation period.

Don't some of her clients feel that she may be intruding on their privacy?

Oh! Many definitely do. That's where her personality comes into play, convincing them that they really do wish to have her help get the important things done. It's her professional aptitude that convinces those who may be suspicious of her agenda when they really need help but wouldn't appreciate the imposition of a stranger offering her the services they so critically call for.

That doesn't seem to be an honorable job for such a professional.

She doesn't actually do the cleaning, shopping and other chores that are required in keeping a household running smoothly. It's her job to evaluate where and what help is needed, than assuring that the proper help is made available through the many organizations that specialize in theses specific services. Among her many functions she refers clients to specialists, including psychologists, doctors, cleaning and aid services, as well as any number of free-loan associations and financial advisors and guides.

You really are proud of your siblings but what about you? You still didn't elaborate on your link in the chain?

Al, you wouldn't find it very interesting, but if you'll give me your phone number I'll speak to my brother. He might get back to you. But your girl friend will have to agree to the interview as well if there are to be any proper results.

Don't worry. Eleanor will go for it. She's my kind of girl. She's just as curious as I am and this can be an interesting experience for both of us. I can be reached at: *** **** *** any time of the day or night.

Next day Al heard the little tune play on his cell phone, notifying him that a call was coming through. "Hello? Who is that calling? I was expecting your call. When can we come over? That sounds great. It will give me an hour to pick up Eleanor. Where do you say we meet? Fine, we'll see you soon"

At four o'clock the door opened just as Al was about to ring the bell. It seems that Rabbi Gill Oberman was just as interested to meet them as they were to meet the rabbi.

Hello, Al, Eleanor, welcome, come on in and get out of the rain. We can park your umbrella in that little bucket in the corner. That's it. Now we can retire to my library. It will be most comfortable there. What will you have to drink, coffee, tea or cold soda? I'm afraid I have nothing a bit stronger than that at hand.

For the present, I'm all right. Do you want something Eleanor?

No thank you, not right now.

By the way you gave us your name as Al, but that must be a contraction. What's your full name?

Allen Fund, but nobody goes to that much trouble anymore, so it became Al.

So you wish to have me psychoanalyze both of you at one sitting. First of all something about the differential in your names is problematic. But that's not the main reason for your visit. From what my brother Dill tells me, you wish to get married in such a way that you'll never have to use his services. That's the way he introduced the subject. He's got a great sense of humor and a way with words, but he's not on the psychoanalyst's couch right now, you are.

One of my methods of observing personal interaction between a prospective bride and groom is by getting them to discuss some subjects that can be controversial. In your case, not being Jewish gets in the way of my usual approach. I can't very well have you arguing about kosher food and the problems that can come up in even the most stringent kitchen as the place and use of various utensils can inadvertently get mixed up. Having you argue about whether you would sneak a ride to the beach on the *Shabbat* while your wife was going to pay you a surprise visit at the door of the synagogue and your not being there is also not a valid topic. Discussing family purity is also not a subject that would impress you. So what I can do is to give you an introductory run down about what Jewish family life is all about.

But first let's discuss your names. They are not compatible. I don't know if you, Eleanor, would really wish to do so but because the Hebrew numerical value of Eleanor is 298, while Allan is 81. That's way out of kilter. So if you, Eleanor really love Allen and wish to show it, you should officially change your name to Ellen, and in that way it would also have a numerical value of 81. That would be the first step in achieving a balance towards a successful marriage.

Since you're both here, please allow me to give you a short introduction to Jewish family life.

The level of religious observance varies amongst Jews of different denominations

Even within the different affiliations, personal religious observances vary and the needs of each Jewish familial unit can differ widely. This depends upon the background and aspirations of each one of the individuals.

I'll deal principally with Orthodoxy where the level of observance and interpretation of Jewish law are stricter than with others. You, who are both not Jewish may find it to be extreme. But it might be enlightening for you

Families are the building block of society and Jewish law and tradition highlights the centrality of the Jewish family unit. Judaism recognizes that each parent has something different to give to their children towards contributing their religious, educational, emotional, social and material needs. It is also important that both parents share the responsibility to give their children 'quality' time. Certain commandments are incumbent on men, while the woman is responsible for others. A child may only have a full Jewish experience if he or she witnesses both the mother and father practicing Judaism.

Where only one parent is Jewish, achieving a full Jewish experience is much more challenging, and even far from ideal.

Jewish tradition highlights the importance of family ties and only by both parents maintaining mutual contact with the child will he be able to sustain positive relationships with both sets of grandparents and other relatives.

It is important for children to be able to experience life cycle events; their own, those of relatives and those within the community. This will be facilitated by exposure to family and social networks of both parents. These events should include weddings, circumcisions, *bar mitzvahs* and *bat mitzvahs* when a Jewish child comes of age; (13 for a boy and 12 for a girl) at which time they take on the responsibilities of being an adult.

What kind of responsibilities are you talking about? I'm sure you don't advocate his participation in supporting the family financially. Not at the expense of his schooling!

Heaven forbid! His or her responsibility is more towards the relationship between him and the creator, as well as his personal behavior between himself and his fellow man.

From the day following his attaining the age of thirteen years of age he is responsible for his actions and either acquires merits or loses points in accord with his performing righteous deeds or sinning.

Boys are recognized as full members of the community at 13 when they celebrate *bar mitzvah*. When girls reach this stage at 12 they celebrate their *bat mitzvah*. Both boys and girls have a period of intense study during the years leading up to the occasion when they accept personal responsibility for all their actions. No longer can their misdeeds be blamed on their being "only children"

Children usually attend *Shabbat* services regularly with their parents. In orthodox communities boys, in particular, accompany their fathers in order to become accustomed to the Synagogue and the prayers. From the age of eight or even younger, every boy is encouraged to spend some tome each morning in prayer. In this way by the time he reaches the age of 13 he will be well enough versed in the prayers to even lead the worshippers during his Bar mitzvah *Shabbat* prayers and read from the Torah scroll before the entire congregation, This is when he has reached the age of total responsibility and is entrusted to enwrap his left arm and head with *Tephilin* during prayers on every week day.

What if he misses a day here or there? Is that so serious?

Once he has passed this milestone in his life, there is no excuse. He is obliged to continue. No turning back and no slowing-down once he's on the fast lane. Only under extenuating circumstances may he miss a day. That is if he is so seriously ill that he simply cannot fulfill this religious obligation, or if he finds himself far from his *Tephilin* (while being delayed in traveling, for instance).

Now getting back to the subject, one of the most serious set of rules that a Jew must follow concerns observance of the *Shabbat* and Festivals.

The *Shabbat* is of particular importance in a Jewish home. Jewish law compels Jews to refrain from various acts of "work" on the *Shabbat*, in commemoration of G-d's day of rest on the seventh day of creation. The main prohibited acts of "work" number thirty-nine and include traveling (other than on foot), cooking, writing, carrying throughout the public domain or into a private domain, the switching on and off of electricity, using a telephone and any transaction of a commercial nature such as shopping.

By lighting two candles, the woman of the house declares that *Shabbat*, or the festival has officially been inaugurated as far as she is concerned, and she cannot be expected to perform any more work. Men still have about 15 to 30 minutes to correct anything that may have not been completed till then.

Festival laws are, for these purposes, almost indistinguishable from *Shabbat* laws except for the labors involved in preparing freshly cooked or baked foods.

I'm sorry to interrupt you again, but I know that one of my Jewish neighbors is very strict yet I notice that his electric lights are on during the evening on Friday, but suddenly go out as the night progresses. That doesn't seem to jive with what you just told us.

I'm happy that you're paying attention to my narrative. A number of activities may be preprogrammed prior to the onset of the *Shabbat* and Festivals. One of them is setting up a time clock to control preset actions during the Holy days. Another preparation is performed so that, even when cooking is forbidden, foods will be kept warm till it is to be consumed, by pacing them on a "hot-plate" and covering them with a blanket, before the *Shabbat* begins. That is considered to be allowable and aids in enjoying warm foods during the *Shabbat*.

When I talk about *Shabbat* observance, festival observance is included.

The Shabbat begins on Friday at "sun-down" about an hour before nightfall or (depending upon the local practice) 15 to 30 minutes before dusk, usually referred to as "sunset". Thus, a practicing Jew must leave work, school or anywhere else, in sufficient time to arrive home by the onset of *Shabbat* which in midwinter, can be quite early and is in force for approximately 25 hours from whatever time it commences, or till three medium size stars are clearly visible in the sky the next night.

Like the *Shabbat*, the festivals also always commence before dusk on the previous day and the same restrictions apply for 25 hours. Family members and guests who intend spending the *Shabbat* or festival together must be in the place where they wish to spend the Shabbat or festival unless they live within walking distance. Festivals can fall on any day of the week but it is extremely unusual for all festive days to fall on weekdays in the same year. Every year the dates will be different as they are governed by the lunar calendar.

That seems strange. While everything is so stringently organized how can it be that dates of the festivals can be so varied from year to year?

The lunar calendar and solar calendar have different cycles, requiring seven extra months to be added to the lunar year every nineteen years. Therefore the dates of festivals are altered from year to year. The holidays are governed by the lunar cycle, while the agricultural year is subject by the solar cycle. Since the *Pessach* festival must always be celebrated in the springtime, such adjustments are made to the calendar during the month prior to *Pessach*.

In addition to the *Shabbat* days, in the Diaspora, there are a total of 13 holy days, while the number of "festivals" in the Jewish calendar in

Israel total eight days annually, including *Yom Kippur*. In addition we also celebrate 11 (9 in the Diaspora) intermediate days that are considered semi-festive in nature and in observance.

In Israel the annual cycle of festivals begins with *Pessach* during March and/or April with two festive days separated by five semi-festive days.

Shavuot during May or June is in force for one day.

Rosh Hashana, "Days of Awe" falls in September or October for two days.

Yom Kippur, also known as a "Day of Awe" falls in September or October for one day.

Sukkot falls during September or October for two days separated by 6 semi festive days.

There are also 5 fast days in addition to *Yom Kippur*, which though it is a day spent in fasting is also considered to be a festive day.

Isn't that a strange way to put it? If it's a day spent in fasting, how can it be considered a festive day?

A good question, but the spiritual nature of the day is such that fasting on this day, a day when Jews confidently anticipate full atonement and forgiveness for all transgressions that might have been performed during the past year, eating is too base a thing to be of any importance. Jews are on a high and food is not a priority at such a time.

It is difficult to adequately stress the centrality and the binding nature of *Shabbat* and festival laws for observant orthodox Jews. *Shabbat* observance in many ways is the central rock on which the rest of Judaism is founded. For an observant Jew there can be no compromise and there is no mechanism for granting dispensation. The only relaxation is where there is a possible risk to life and so, when family members require emergency medical attention, they can travel or phone for medical assistance on *Shabbat* and festivals.

In addition there are the following: days of thanksgiving;

Hanukah in November or December lasts 8 days, and travel or works are not restricted.

Tu B'Shvat February or March—new year for the fruit trees.

Purim during February or March for one day without travel or work restrictions.

Yom Ha'atzmaut—in the month of May for one day spent celebrating independence.

Yom Yerushalayim—during May or June, the day Jerusalem was reunited.

Lag B'omer—May or June is a break in the solemnity during counting the omer days.

Tu B'Av a day of joy for a number of historical events that took place on that date.

May I please ask another question?

Certainly, go ahead.

You just enumerated seven times for thanksgiving. Seven days without nearly any restrictions. Against them I counted, and I hope I counted correctly, seven Festive days. Is there any special significance between them?

Till now, I hadn't realized the relationship in such a way. I'm afraid I can't enlighten you on the matter till I've had a chance to research the phenomena. Now I see that what the Jewish sages of old have advocated is so true, when they said, "From all my teachings have I learned, even more so, from my students."

Getting back to my narration, let's go back to the beginning. Life begins with the birth of a child.

At the age of eight days or as soon as possible thereafter, if there are medical reasons for delay, the father is obligated to circumcise his male children during a ceremony called *brit mila*. Since most men are not well enough versed in the operation the circumcision is carried out by a *mohel* who is registered to carry out this procedure, having been authorized following stringent examination by the rabbinate. As the boy's name is not announced until completion of the circumcision, they are named at this ceremony.

If the boy is a firstborn to the mother by normal birth, he is formally redeemed in the presence of a *Kohen* at 30 days of age during a ceremony known as *pidyon haben*. This redemption is obligatory and is done at a cost of five silver *Sheqalim* transferred to the *Kohen* in exchange for the first born boy, known as a *Bechor*.

On a boy's third birthday some families will arrange for his first haircut in a ceremony known as a *Halaka*. This is a rite of passage where he is immediately introduced to a religious education. This is also when he is supposed to be old enough to understand personal cleanliness. He dons a *Talit Katan* with *tzitzit* and begins to wear a head covering constantly.

Girls are usually named in the synagogue following her birth, often on the first day that the torah is read.

All these events are causes for congregational and family celebration.

I'm sorry to disturb you, Rabbi, but can I have that cup of coffee? I can get it myself if you'll just tel me where the makings are.

Certainly. But I'd prefer to be present so as to ascertain that the dairy cups and spoons don't become mixed up with the meat dishes.

Thank you, but I really don't want you to go to any trouble about it.

No problem . . .

Now getting back to my lecture; weddings between two Jews can take place at any venue; in a synagogue a private home or a wedding hall. Some have even taken place on the beach or even in sports' arenas.

The officiating Rabbi must ensure that religious law is followed and that the marriage is a permitted one according to Jewish law prior to the wedding being celebrated. There are times of sorrow within the Jewish calendar when weddings are not celebrated.

The groom validates the marriage by presenting his bride with an item that he personally owns, usually a plain gold ring.

In addition to a marriage certificate, the parties will receive a religious marriage document called the *ketubah*, which belongs to the wife. This document is signed by two Jewish witnesses to the marriage, who are in no way related to either of the couple. It is prepared; guaranteeing her predetermined monetary compensation should her husband predecease or divorce her.

It will have to be produced upon application for a religious divorce ('*get*'). It may also be required as proof of the Jewish identity of any child born of that marriage.

A central theme of marital life is that of family purity. As part of a complete intimate relationship, the couple is expected to refrain from physical contact at certain times of the wife's monthly cycle and then she should attend a ritual bath (the *mikveh*) before resuming their relationship.

If a married man dies childless; his brother (if any) must perform a ceremony called *chalitza* before a Beth Din to enable the widow to remarry. Until then, the widow is forbidden to remarry. In any event, no widow or divorcee may marry within 90 days of the death of or legal separation from her husband.

At weddings, both parents of a bride and groom usually stand with their child during the marriage ceremony under the marriage *chupah*. Grandparents are often also honored by their presence under the *chupah*.

When death finally catches up, hopefully at old age, and after having led a full and productive life, Jews are usually buried as soon as possible after death. This is most often on the actual day or night of the death, although a day or two later is possible if family members are definitely coming from abroad. This means that usually there is very little notice of a family funeral. There are special rules for the preparation of the body for burial carried out by the *chevra kadisha* burial society. As little interference with the body as possible is a very important requirement, so a post mortem is stringently discouraged unless absolutely necessary although an MRI scan may be accepted if there may be extenuating circumstances that require such an examination.

If a body is cremated some orthodox cemeteries will not bury the ashes, as they are held to be as repulsive as are the remains of an apostate.

After the funeral, the immediate family of the deceased, meaning spouse, parents, children and siblings, mourn for seven days. This is known as the *shiva*. During this time the members of the immediate family stay at home, sit on low chairs and receive visitors and condolences. During the thirty days following a death, men do not shave or cut their hair. Attendance at a synagogue for prayer is practiced thrice daily. There are additional restrictions and requirements that extend to certain mourners for up to a year from date of the death. These include attending joyous occasions, and parties where music is played.

While Judaism is not a proselytizing religion, conversions are carried out by courts of Jewish religious law (*Batei Din*). Each *Beth Din* has different arrangements and not all foreign or even Israeli conversions are necessarily universally accepted. If a woman converts to Judaism after the birth of a child, the child must be converted in his/her own right. If a non-Jewish child is adopted, the child will need to be converted and in the case of a boy a circumcision must take place. In such cases circumcision cannot take place until the adoption process is complete.

Divorce as an option: Nowhere within Jewish law is it stated that marriage is a lifelong union. Judaism recognizes that marriages, unhappily, can fail and consequently provides specifically for divorce so that parties are free to remarry. However a divorce is not initiated by the woman, though she must agree to accept the divorce document.

'Get' is the Hebrew term for a Jewish divorce. A Jewish divorce is a consensual document dissolving the marriage. The process is administered by the *Beth Din*. Traditionally the 'get' may only be granted by the husband to the wife who in turn accepts it. It is a formal document hand written on parchment on the instructions of the husband. After the giving and receiving of a 'get' both parties are free to marry again in a Jewish ceremony although the wife has to wait 90 days before remarriage (excluding the day of receiving the 'get' and the day of remarriage) or 24 months from the birth of any child.

Why is it so important to obtain a 'get'?

If a married Jewish woman who does not have a 'get' bears children by another Jewish man, those children will have the status of *mamzer* (illigitimate). Such children suffer considerable problems when it comes to their marriage and are very limited in their choice of partner.

It is of the utmost importance that a Jewish woman, especially one of childbearing age going through divorce proceedings, should be sure have a 'get'. This is because if a wife subsequently wishes to obtain a 'get', the husband may not then be willing to grant one or it may not be possible to find him or because of mental impairment he may lack the capacity voluntarily to grant a 'get'. There is no remedy for any of these situations. Therefore it is essential that a wife is advised of these pitfalls.

Traditionally the procedure for a 'get' must be initiated by the husband. He instructs a trained scribe to write the 'get'. The specifically written document is given by the husband to the wife in the presence of two witnesses. The act of the wife accepting the document completes the divorce process. Arrangements can be made so that an agent can deliver the document on behalf of the husband to the wife so that the couple need not meet. There are no references to responsibility for the breakdown of the marriage and no blame or fault

The actual 'get' document is retained by the Beth Din for safekeeping but a certificate of proof or release (p'tur) is given to both parties which needs to be produced if either wishes to remarry under Jewish law.

The modern fact of cohabitation without marriage is acknowledged although not encouraged and in most observant orthodox communities, couples do not cohabit.

Marriage is arranged with the consent of both parties and may often take place at a young age, sometimes even at 17 or 18 years of age.

Should a couple cohabit as man and wife and for instance children are born of that relationship they may require a 'get'.

If, before a 'get' is given, a woman cohabits with a man or has sexual intercourse with a man she will be regarded as an adulterer and may not marry that man according to Jewish law, even if a 'get' is later obtained, unless the 'get' has first been obtained. She will also lose the compensation agreed upon in the Ketuba.

The role of Rabbis is often more extensive than that of pastoral teacher and mediator. They decide questions of Jewish law and may act as an arbitrator. If a Rabbi is asked a question on Jewish law, his answer binds the questioner. Some communities turn to the Rabbi or the Jewish court (the Beth Din) for determination of civil issues, including inheritance, in preference to the civil courts.

As for prayer, adult men and boys over the age of 13 pray three times a day, in the morning, afternoon and in the evening. Whilst this can be performed individually, observant orthodox Jews prefer to attend synagogue and pray with a quorum consisting of at least 10 adult men. Such group prayer is particularly important when a person is in a period of mourning. The comparatively short afternoon prayer may take place anytime between shortly after noon till dusk.

While evening prayers take place after three stars are visible in the sky.

The emphasis on education in Judaism has great prominence on the duty to educate children. Many families will prioritize time and funds for their children's higher education

Jews are required to eat only kosher food. This means that while all fruit, vegetables and grains are permitted after having been examined to assure that they are not infested, only certain meat, fish and poultry are permitted. Jews who observe the dietary laws (including religious slaughter laws) require all processed foods (including cheese and wine) to be under rabbinical supervision in order to be satisfied that no prohibited ingredients have been used. Consequently vegetarian cooked food may also be refused. There are strict additional rules for the preparation and serving of food even at home including separation of meat and milk products and utensils.

Dairy and meat may not be prepared together nor eaten together, even at the same meal. In fact, according to different levels of observance, one must wait anywhere from three to six hours after consuming meat dishes before eating any dairy product. Fish and meat are never eaten together. Every Jewish home has separate sets of pots, pans, dishes and cutlery for meat and dairy meals.

What happens if some diverse utensils get mixed up?

I see that you are very attentive. When metal utensils get mixed up, they can be koshered. The degree of heat whereby the pot or spoon absorbs would be sufficient for it to discharge what it has absorbed. So by superheating water in a larger vessel where this utensil has been placed can rectify the situation.

Superheat? What do you mean by that? Water boils at 100 degrees centigrade and cannot be heated over that.

In addition to heating the water, a piece of steel is heated separately to a higher degree. It is then dropped into the boiling vessel by means of pliers, which in turn superheats the water.

However if the mix-up has been with crockery there is no choice but to break the dish. Glass can be koshered by soaking in water for three days, changing the water each day.

Wow! So even if everything is so stringent some situations can be rectified. Is this a common procedure?

Only when the householder knows what it's all about, can he perform these procedures, but most do.

Pessach dishes and utensils must also be different from those used during the rest of the year. This is during the week when all or any leaven including bread or any other kind of *Hametz* is prohibited from being even kept in the house.

As for clothing, observant Jewish men keep our heads covered at all times generally by wearing a hat or *kippah*. It is common to have strings called tzizit hanging from one of the items of clothing, known as a *talit katan*. During prayer we wear a larger oblong garment over the shoulders, a *tallit* that also has *tzitzit* affixed to it. Observant orthodox married women cover their hair or wear a wig at all times in public. Observant orthodox women and girls will only wear modest clothing and many will not wear trousers, short skirts or short sleeves.

That Kosher coffee was great. But your narration about the Jewish culture was even more fascinating. I never imagined that life could be so interesting, even with so many rules and regulations.

Though I still have another question, since nothing resembling "work" may be performed on *Shabbat*, isn't it awfully boring? No driving, no TV, no telephone conversations. How can one get any pleasure during the entire day?

On the contrary. That is the best part of the entire week. That is when we enjoy each other's company, conversing amongst ourselves, spending real quality time with our children and other members of the family without the stress of the work week. That is the time we can relax and even grab a restful nap without feelings of guilt at "wasting" valuable productive time. That is the time when we can open a book and read or study. The three meals that we eat on *Shabbat* are unhurried, interspersed with conversation and songs sung by all the participants. Children also take an integral part in these events, where they show what they've learned during the week. *Shabbat* is the greatest invention in the world.

The way you explained that makes me wonder how we non-Jews are so always on the go, at the expense of the best thing in life. We never relax. I wonder how we actually survive the stressful life we lead. I like the idea of a total cessation of all the mundane activities for a full day, but doubt if I could actually get used to such a way of life.

That was only an introduction. Many years are spent studying and learning the intricacies behind all the commandments. Not everything is cut and dried. We have much flexibility built into the Jewish religion. Certain situations arise when we must improvise and correct problems. Agricultural crops must be tithed before they may be consumed. There are certain years when part of the tithes must be distributed to the poor.

But during the seventh year of the septennial cycle all fruits and vegetables are free of tithes. It takes a lot of study to even begin understanding these finer points.

One never finishes his Jewish education. The deeper one delves into the subject the deeper we find ourselves digging for more intricate information. Not even 120 years is sufficient to graduate from our school.

You know something, Rabbi Gill. I find that the Jewish religion, with all the strict rules and regulations to be fascinating and wish to learn more about it. I'd even like to become a Jew. No. Let's put it this way, I wish to become Jewish and lead a Jewish life.

Turning to his fiancée he asked, Ellen, what about you? Do you see yourself wearing a wig and celebrating a full day of rest on *Shabbat*?

I was hoping you'd see it that way too, Allen. No question about it. I wish to get married as a Jew and lead a Jewish life.

What do you say Rabbi, would you prepare us for conversion?

I'm supposed to discourage you from taking such a drastic step. The commitment may be too much for you, and you're not speaking only for yourself, but for both of you.

What kind of life have we been leading anyway? Since we are about to make such a drastic change by accepting each other's foibles. We might as well take the giant step and become Jews. The lifestyle really appeals to me.

It would take a lot of time and effort on your part, but let's put it this way . . .

That's another story.

GLOSSARY

Av	The fifth month in the Jewish calendar, beginning with Nissan
Bar Mitzvah	When a boy reaches thirteen years of age
Bat Mitzvah	When a girl reaches twelve years of age
Bechor	First born male
Bet Din (Batei Din)	Rabbinical courts
Brit mila	Circumcision of a male child on the eighth day after birth
Get	Divorce document
Halaka	First hair cut for a boy, usually at age three
Hametz	Leaven—prohibited during the week of *Pessach*
Ketuba	Marriage contract
Kippa	A skull cap
Kohen	One who would serve in the Holy temple when it exists
Lag B'Omer	The 33rd day of counting the days of *Omer*
Mamzer	A child born as a result of an incestuous relationship
Mohel	Circumciser
Nissan	The first month of the Jewish year—falls in the springtime
Omer	The day when we celebrate harvest of the new grains
Pessach	A springtime festival during which all leaven is prohibited

Pidion Haben	Redemption of a first born Israelite male
Purim	A joyous day spent feasting and exchanging gifts
Rosh Hashana	The annual New year
Shabbat	The seventh day of the week, the Sabbath
Shavuot	A one day festival, 50 days after the beginning of *Pessach*
Sheqalim	Unit of Israeli money
Sukkot	We dwell in temporary booths for one week
Talit	Prayer shawl worn during prayer
Talit Katan	Smaller than a *Talit*, worn all day under the shirt
Tephilin	Phylacteries, worn on the left arm and head during prayers
Tu B'Av	The fifteenth day of the month of *Av*—of many happy events
Tu B'Shvat	Arbor day—the new year of the trees
Tzitzit	Fringes tied to the four corners of a *Talit* and *Talit Katan*
Yom Ha'atzmaut	Israel's independence day
Yom Kippur	A day spent in prayer while fasting, a day of atonement
Yom Yerushalayim	The day Jerusalem was reunited after nearly 2000 years

THE FACT IN FICTION

This is a fictionalized account of what could have really been a factual situation. The plot came to me in a dream during the night of Friday/Saturday on the *Shabbat* portion "*Yitro*" of the year 5772. A few facts are real but most is fictionalized.

Upon awakening from a restful sleep I had a nagging hunch that there must be a message to be learned from such a vivid dream. As soon as the Shabbat was over on Saturday night, checking data stored on my computer, I sought some reasonable explanation for having so lucidly remembered that dream. For some inexplicable reason, I followed my inclination and opened the page describing my paternal great-grandfather's family on my comprehensive family tree of more than 2,000 names.

My grandfather BenZion is listed as first-born (1874), followed by a younger brother Hersh-Ber, who I had known during my youthful years, after which follow the names of three sisters. One un-named brother (probably born in 1887 or so) identified as a "son (stayed in Europe)." Their youngest sister Hayia Riva completes the generation of my grandfather and his siblings.

I had never paid much attention to the young son, who only bore the notation that he remained in Europe. The youngest sister, though not noted in such a derogatory manner, also remained in Europe, but I have record of her marriage there with a listing of her descendents. The older two brothers and their families all immigrated to Canada, settling in Montreal prior to the First World War. I have no specific information about the three middle sisters, as their destinies are not intimated.

One of the youngest sister's three daughters, who following some thirty-five years of widowhood, was later married to my grandfather, her uncle, as his second wife, becoming my "step-grandmother". Her grandson lives in our neighborhood. We still pray together in the same synagogue and know each other quite well. But that is not an integral part of this account.

I am a firm believer that dreams include serious clues to natural events and am infatuated with the idea that there may be some fact within this fiction, and that I may yet be able to prove, beyond any reasonable doubt that the "son who stayed in Europe" actually did leave a trail bordering on reality.

Shmuel Shimshoni

CHAPTER I

It was quite unnerving to feel a gentle tap my left shoulder. Before I completed a quarter turn in the direction of the touch he called me by my given, as well as my family name.

Upon completion of a swivel in his direction I found myself confronted by an unfamiliar face. One I could have sworn that I'd never glimpsed before. He might have been anywhere from twenty to sixty, but age wasn't a factor. The voice was not familiar, neither was his accent. Yet there was some semblance of amity in it; some line, shape of an earlobe, nose-tip or curl to the ends of his lips. Some inherent characteristic was evident that reminded me of someone I might have known, if even for a fleeting moment. Even if I had never known who, probably someone I might have had some relationship with in the distant past.

However I was certain that I'd never laid eyes upon this stranger, yet he knew my name. He knew who I was, and his tone that implied that I should be cognizant of whom he was.

At the time, I'd been contemplating something that I considered important, but as a result of this startling encounter, I was totally distracted from the reverie wherein I'd been so thoroughly absorbed up until that moment. As my attention was disrupted I completely lost my original line of thought. It disturbed me no end because I was sure it was significant, but I can not recall what it was that I considered so interesting a subject.

Encounters of this type rarely happen to ordinary people and I don't consider myself to be anything but ordinary.

For a moment I was disconcerted, between wishing to return to my inner thoughts and the inclination to satisfy my curiosity about whom this individual was and why he approached me altogether. What did he wish to gain by making himself known to me and why at this particular inappropriate moment?

I was so flustered by this encounter that, though it only happened less than a couple of days ago, try as I might, I still can't recall at what time of day it occurred, as if that really would make a difference.

While trying to figure out how to enter into a conversation with him I intently studied his face. From the conflicting color tone between the front of his neck and that of his deeply tanned forehead I gathered that he spent a lot of time, not lying on the beach, but walking around during the day. The indentations on the bridge of his nose proved that, up until quite recently, he had been wearing glasses. If they had been sun-glasses his approach to me must have been during the daylight hours. Then again it could even have been at night when he made his presence known, and it might have been mandatory for him to wear glasses only while driving, so he might have removed them after parking his vehicle. Then again there was no discernable difference in the skin color around his eyes, so he was probably not a habitual sun-glass wearer. I felt particularly proud of myself for reaching such a conclusion all by myself about his wearing glasses and only temporarily.

He bore a pleasant smile that showed a set of gleaming white teeth. His philtrum was hidden behind a well trimmed mustache and his well groomed light brown hair was partially covered by a knitted blue *kippa* that repetitiously bore a single embroidered word in bright yellow yarn around its circumference. It read *Dan,* but in Hebrew letters, running from right to left. This is what gave me a hint about his name.

"Dan", I addressed him. "How do you know me? And how did you find me?"

"It took a lot of research to find you, Shmuel. But even though you changed your family name at last we meet."

"Dan, what do we have in common that made it worth your while to seek me out?"

"Shmuel, I'm not only surprised, but disappointed. You, the only member of your generation, who spends so much time and effort in compiling your comprehensive family tree so thoroughly, yet never paid much attention to my position on your charts."

"Since you seem to have been doing such deep research yourself, in order to have located me, you should also be aware that putting together a family chart is a never ending job. There are always some loose vines that flutter around between the branches. Some buds show up here and there, while older leaves wrinkle up and fly away with the slightest breeze. In my project, you might be one of those twigs that I haven't got around to tie in with the rest. So please don't feel overlooked by my lack of attention to your position in the family. That is if you really fit in"

"That's okay; I just wanted to get your attention about where I tie in with your family."

"Dan, I suggest we sit down at the computer. I think it would be a good place to begin. We have a few things to discuss and that's where I can get to the data with a few clicks. But Dan, what's your family name? You haven't introduced yourself yet".

"Uh? Oh yes. It's Ben-Tzvi, and I live in Zichon Yaacov. That's been our family residence for over ninety years".

"Oh! That's not far from here".

CHAPTER II

I'll start be showing you what I do have, and then you can help me fill in the gaps. I have some old photos of my ancestors, who might be yours, as well:

My great-grandmother
Sarah Dina Cohen

My great-grandfather
Alter Hershcu Halevi

Their children were:

BenZion	Hersh-Ber	Frima	Miriam	Gittel	Son	Hayia Riva
Born	Born				Probably	Married
28/04/1874	Romania				born	**Moshe**
Romania					In 1887	Sakaju
Married	Married				(stayed in	Their
Mindel	**Malka**				Europe)	daughter
1898						**Raisel**
						Married
						Michael
						Greenberg

then	Then
Raisel	**BenZion**
18/05/1953	18/05/1953
in	In
Bnei Brak	Bnei Brak

Okay Dan, now it's your turn to show me how you relate to the family, or do I have to go back any further?

CHAPTER III

"No, Shmuel that's just right. I can't put any light on any of the three middle sisters, but I can surely tell you all about my great-grandfather who left us a legacy. He seems to have been listed as "Son" but that's an error. His name was "Ben" and that was erroneously translated as son.

"You know Dan? I never considered that entry to be a mistaken translation. An intriguing observation, though."

"Another odd thing is that your grandfather was named BenZion, though the family was probably very anti-Zionistic. When my great-grandfather, Ben became involved with Hovivai Zion while in his teens, the rest of the family shunned him. That is probably why he was singled out with the notation that he remained in Europe. Their sisters who also stayed behind when the two older brothers left Europe, where not referred to in so derogatory a manner.

So it seems that after BenZion and Hersh-Ber went to Canada, they didn't keep in contact with Ben, and so, were unaware that he also left Romania and made his way to Palestine. His resources were quite meager and much of the trip he made was over land via Turkey, and on towards The Land of Israel by boat through the port of Jaffo.

He joined up with a group of other young Zionists. Of the five he was eighteen years of age when he left Pode-Leoi in 1905. Only one of the others was older than he. They met in for the first time in the closest city Yassy where they planned their journey and collected some supplies. From there made their way south towards Bulgaria. Figuring that the cost of commercial transportation would exceed their budget and by making their way on foot, accommodations along the way would exceed their pooled money, they bought a horse and wagon for the trip.

Making good time even though they were careful not to over-strain their mare and being early summer they were able to spend their nights camping among the trees in the many forests that they traversed, along the way. To their good fortune no rain fell. That in itself buoyed up their spirits during those couple of weeks. Leaving the southern border of Bulgaria brought them to Eastern Rumelia further to the south.

It was not till they reached the Turkish border where they were stopped and questioned about their destination. They had been warned not to even intimate that Palestine was on their agenda, even though it was part of the Ottoman Empire as from time to time Jewish immigration was blocked. Fortunately each one of the five had been pre-trained with a vocation and carried the basic tools of their trades along with them. In this way they convinced the authorities that they would not become burdensome on the government, but were capable of supporting themselves while seeking their fortune in Turkey.

Naphtali was a shoemaker, a trade that was in high demand; Fishel, a tailor, Berel was a tinsmith; the Moshe was an experienced cook. My great-grandfather Ben was an accomplished cabinet maker.

In order prevent suspicion that they were on their way to Palestine, when they got to Constantinople they sold their horse and wagon, rented cheap living quarters together and fanned out in the city to seek out work possibilities and were all successful in finding employment. Given their, much in demand trades they had no trouble finding jobs and very quickly organized themselves, earning money and saving as much as they could for the next lap of their journey. The cook who worked part-time in a hotel took care of running the house, shopping and cooking their meals.

Ben had an uncanny way of quickly analyzing any situation and, with his stubborn streak he made split-second decision that though might have seemed unpopular at first, eventually proved to be correct. In this way he was accepted as the leader of the group, even though he was not the senior member.

From the time they had left Yassy they had no contact with any local member of the Hovevai Zion organization, who had instructed about how to behave in order to achieve their common goal. One of the most important directives was to keep a low profile, be pleasant with neighbors without becoming too friendly. Government spies were aplenty and they always sought out suspicious activities.

When a few days had passed by, and after unceremoniously wandering around the neighborhood wherein they had chosen to dwell they located a small synagogue within easy walking distance from their flat and attended daily prayer sessions. They felt that they would be able to be a bit more at ease and gleaned information about where they could depend upon kosher food sources without relying on a vegetarian diet.

After some two months one of the congregants approached them and intimated that if they sought information about Palestine he would be happy to introduce them to the right party. At first it seemed to be an interesting development in their search for some contact with the right parties, but on the other hand it might have been a trap by the authorities to stymie their plans for Alyiah. Ben took the initiative in carrying on the conversation and found that the stranger's brusque approach had been too suspicious. With finesse, so as to avoid any hint of their motive, he gently steered the discussion towards sports and their keen interest in the successes of the Turkish national football team. They wished to meet with the team manager. "Could you arrange that for us"?

His wariness proved correct, especially when the stranger then showed a total disinterest in continuing the discussion. That plan had been one of those worked out by their counselor before they left Romania. If the real contact would have continued the conversation along the lines of sport, but switching to talk about skiing, even though it was mid summer, it would have been a sign that the contact might be trustworthy.

Some time passed and members of the group were still biding their time, working daily at the jobs they had found and by pooling their earnings, were building up a sum that would aid them in the next lap of their journey. The next part of their trip would be much more expensive than their first stage that got them this far.

Meanwhile they immediately changed to a different congregation where, though the attendants were fewer in number. They were amicable but not too inquisitive. In fact they were very happy to have so many new members in regular attendance thereby bolstering the quorum that till then seemed to be quite weak during the week-day morning sessions

On a Saturday night when the congregants gathered under the crystal clear sky where stars twinkled brightly, while the half moon showed that a quarter of the Hebrew month had been passed, the time had come to bless the new moon, as is the custom during the second week of each month. The reciprocal greeting "Shalom Alaychem—Alaycem Shalom" was being animatedly exchanged between members of the congregation when along with the greeting by one member of the company a note was surreptitiously passed into Ben's hand. Ben hadn't got even a glimpse of the one whom passed it on to him, but furtively slipped the folded sheet between the pages of the prayer book that he'd been holding in his right hand, to be retrieved later while returning the book to the bookshelf at the completion of the ceremony.

At last contact was being made.

CHAPTER IV

Ben could hardly wait to return to the flat that they called home in order to examine the note that was burning a hole in his pocket. His room-mates had never seen Ben so agitated. He had always been calm. No stressful situation had so perturbed his demeanor during the months that they had been together. What had he seen or heard that made him so anxious?

As soon as one of them had performed the *Havdala,* sipped some wine and extinguished the candle Ben ceremoniously whipped out the memo and carefully unfolded it with shaking hands, just staring at the words for a few seconds trying to absorb their significance. One of the others took the letter from Ben and began to read out the message that had been scribbled in Hebrew. In essence it advised them that they were being invited to attend a special meeting with an emissary of Hovivai Zion.

בס"ד
חבריה,
הנכם מוזמנים לפגישה דחופה בנוגע המשך עלייתכם ארצה.
על הראשון מחמישתכם שלכם להגיע לחנות לבגדי גברים על רחוב סברג'
מספר 43 הלילה בשעה עשר בדיוק. הדלת האחורי לא תהיה נעולה.
עליכם לבוא <u>בהפרש של שתי דקות</u> בין זה לזה. בכניסה יש להיכנס לתא
ההלבשה האמצעי, לסגור את הדלת – ולאחר כן ללחוץ על דופן האחורי, שגם
היא דלת אל אולם הפגישה.
עתידכם תלוי בשמירה בדייקנות את ההיראות אלו.
חזקי

In translation, it read—"You are all invited to attend an urgent meeting regarding the next step in your *Alyiah* At exactly ten o'clock tonight the first one of you is to come to the men's' clothing store on Savredge Street number 43. The rear door will be unlocked.

You are each to enter separately, <u>two minutes apart</u>. Upon entry you should each enter the middle try-on cubicle and close the door, after which you are to turn around and push on the rear wall which is also a doorway to the meeting hall. Your future depends upon following these instructions meticulously Signed by Hezki.

Someone checked the time and found that they still had a little over an hour to mentally prepare themselves for the imminent interview that would set them on their way.

The excitement and anticipation of what awaited them was so tense that no one even thought to mention supper.

The location of the men's clothing store at Savredge Street 43, was very popular and not far from their quarters.

Being careful to keep the appointment for what might be the most important cog in reaching their imminent goal, getting to the Land of Israel, they wasted no time.

Moshe quietly opened the rear door of the shop at exactly ten o'clock and being familiar with the layout of the store, because he had done some shopping there already, strode towards the assigned cubicle, entered and closed the door, as instructed. He then turned around and pushed open the wall that swung back on a well oiled pivot. He was greeted by a committee of three Hovevai Zion members, who offered him a seat. Before him were some mugs, an assortment of cookies and a hot kettle of tea, to which he thankfully helped himself.

Hezki introduced himself then asked for his name. When he replied "Moshe", Hezki checked his name against a list that was spread before them on the table. More questions were fired at him: Age? "Twenty-one". Marital status? "Single". Occupation? "Chef". Experience? "Three years cooking on a Ship at sea" What his intended objective? "Continue working in my profession." Had he any preference where to settle? "Either Jerusalem or Jaffa where I can find work in a hotel and will be able to cook only Kosher meals". What was his financial situation? To which he replied, "The entire group of five live together and pool all our earnings. I'm not fully aware of the total, but our treasurer can answer that when he arrives".

By that time the inner door swung open and the tailor entered. He was duly invited to have a seat and help himself to some refreshment that he thankfully accepted. It was his turn to register with Hezki. "Name?" "Fishel". Age? "Seventeen". Marital status? "Single". Occupation? "Tailor". Experience?" "Four years certified apprenticeship". What his intended objective? "Continue working in my profession." Had he any preference where to settle? "I'd like try the new city of Tel Aviv where I can probably find lots of work".

The next one to arrive was the shoemaker who graciously accepted the invitation to have some tea, but refused the cookies, claiming that he preferred not to eat. He was cautious while answering the questions that the others had already had been asked, but was asked a couple of time to "Speak a little louder, please". "Name?" "Naphtali". Age? "Fifteen". Marital status? "Single". Occupation? "Shoemaker". Experience?" "Three and a half years working with my uncle". What his intended objective? "Fixing shoes" Had he any preference where to settle? "I'll work wherever people wear-out shoes".

The tinsmith made his appearance just on schedule and gratefully took his seat right in front of the kettle that was quite hot, its spout still steaming. He helped himself to a mug of tea, added three spoonfuls of sugar and stirred it for more than a minute before taking a preliminary sip to test the, by now tepid liquid. He then added another spoonful of sugar to satisfy his sweet tooth. All eyes were upon him till he seemed satisfied and laid aside the spoon. Now it was his turn to be questioned, as the others had been: "Name?" "Berel". Age? "Seventeen". Marital status? "Single". Occupation? "Tinsmith". Experience?" "Four years". What his intended objective? "To work as a tinsmith". Had he any preference where to settle? "Tel Aviv sounds like a place to find work, with all the new construction going on there".

Finally with a silent motion the door opened and Ben walked in, closing the door to its former position. "The tea may not be hot anymore, but you must be thirsty, so please have some," "That's alright. I see that we are all here, so what have we got to discuss"?

First of all please let me have your name". Ben Hershcu". Age? "Eightteen". Marital status? "Single". Occupation? "Cabinet maker—carpenter". Experience?" "Three and a half years as an apprentice, then one year for a cooper". What his intended objective? "I wish to work with wood". Had he any preference where to settle? "I'd like to try Zichron Yaacov where they always make or fix wooden barrels at the Baron's winery".

"Who is your treasurer"? All eyes turned to Berel. He was somewhat surprised at the question and not quite prepared as to how to reply, but silently raised his right hand to indicate that it was he. "How much money do you have right now in the fund? "We have about 300 Leu, money that we had when we arrived from Romania and 720 Lira with a few Para from our local wages in addition to the 500 lira from the sale of our horse and wagon, when we arrived".

"So that works out to 60 Leu and about 225 Lira or just under 345 Turkish Lira each. I'm afraid that in order to sail from Constantinople to Jaffa you must each have a least 600 Lira in order to cover the necessary fare and baksheesh that is all part of any plan that we can agree upon."

An audible sigh was heard before Ben rose to his feet and asked, "What about making the trip over land through Syria? That must surely be a much cheaper alternative."

"Let me tell you about an actual experience that one family endured with that route . . . ." Just then the door swung open and three excited young ladies came bounding into the meeting hall.

CHAPTER V

Hezki, didn't seem to like the idea and hollered, "Rachel, Shoshana, Pearl! What are you doing here now? Our meeting is supposed to be at eleven".

"The back door was unlocked and we couldn't wait to tell you the good news".

"Well you're disturbing us right now so please leave and return when you're supposed to".

"But I can't wait to tell you. We have it all, and plenty more. We're all ready to go".

"I'm afraid I don't know what you mean. Have all of what"?

"All the money we need".

"But how"?

With an impish grin Shoshana said, "We'll come back later and tell you". Looking around, she noticed our group silently sitting around the table and asked, "Are these guys ready to make the trip also"?

"Shoshana, we'll discuss it later, but yesterday you were short by over a thousand Lira. How did you manage to amass enough money so quickly"?

Meanwhile the five young men were watching the banter, not quite understanding what kind of conversation was going on between Hezki and the shortest of the three girls, the one he addressed as Shoshana, the one with the braided red hair.

"All right, I guess you can stay, now that you're here. I was just about to tell our *Haverim* about a situation that had occurred to a family in their attempt to make the trip over land. You may as well listen as well.

CHAPTER VI

A family of three generations numbering twelve persons, that included a couple of toddlers thought that they would save time and money by making *Alyiah* via Syria and Lebanon.

After leaving Samarqand in Uzbekistan, for some reason they made their way northward to Moscow. After spending about a year in Russia they headed to Odessa, where they boarded a ship to Istanbul. There they spent two years, losing two family members to Typhus and were buried here in Turkey.

They were finally able to continue their journey south from Istanbul including a number of unscheduled stops along the way till they arrived in the city of Allepo in the north-west of Syria, not far from the Turkish-Syrian border. Their arrival was there was quite late on a Friday afternoon and only with the aid of local Jews were they able to arrange some sort of accommodations for *Shabbat*.

The next lap of their journey was by train, but not without utter frustration. Ten people with fourteen bulky packages containing all their worldly possessions impatiently lingered for hours on the railway station platform till a train finally chugged its way along the tracks and came to a stop. The cars were so fully packed with passengers that the conductors refused to open the doors for more travelers.

Upon quickly sizing up the situation one of the young family members clambered aboard through a window of the closest railway car and called for his father to quickly pass up their baggage. Not being aware when the train might pull out again, he continued, frenziedly pulling up every member of the party through the window till they were all miraculously on board. They were crowded but all together, on their way towards the capitol city of Lebanon, Beirut.

When they finally untangled themselves from the train in Beirut the grandfather made a comment concerning that trip that rang so true and remained with the family for many years afterwards. "When one begins a trip he utters a benediction, called A prayer for the way"—and upon reaching his destination he is obliged to recite the *Hagomel* blessing".

In Beirut the grandfather attempted to make arrangements at the Turkish embassy to arrange visas to Palestine but found that due to a Muslim festival it was closed and nobody could tell him when they would reopen to the public. Ramadan could even extend for another few weeks. With patience and resources running dangerously low where does one go to seek solace?

One visits a synagogue where, by chance, he met a fellow Bucharian Jew who also wished to get to the Land of Israel. He convinced the grandfather that they would have little to lose by hiring the services of a smuggler to get them all across the border. Eventually this stranger married into the family.

The night chosen for the perilous journey was moonless. The donkeys that bore them and their personal effects slipped in all directions on the rocky soil. The trees were crowded ever so close seeming to purposely block their progress and the constant fear of being spotted by "shoot-to-kill" patrols was very real. After several hours of slithering, sliding and falling, getting up again and reloading their luggage on the dinky little animals, with dawn quickly approaching, they finally found themselves crossing the northern border of Palestine near the heights of Rosh Hanikra. With the last of their few Liras squeezed out their purse for a final baksheesh to the smuggler, who held their baggage for ransom, they finally reached their goal, The Land of Israel. They might have knelt to kiss the ground but were afraid they wouldn't have the strength to get up again, following such a strenuous expedition

They found themselves penniless, totally fatigued but still days away from their final destination. The first Jew they met along their way sensed their predicament and loaned them enough money to get to Jerusalem where they joined relatives who had already established themselves there.

So, *haverim*, Is that the choice you would make in order to try and save few Liras? This family was fortunate. They might have missed getting on that train in Allepo and wait for days for another, even more crowded one that might, or might not stop altogether. They could have chosen a smuggler who would slit their throats and steal their belongings. They could have been spotted by a trigger-happy patrol, and their bodied left for the wolves, depriving them of even a proper burial. I shudder whenever I recall their unbelievable experiences. After having spent so much time and energy they were on the verge of failure so many times, but sheer perseverance and with the help of the Almighty, they literally experienced miracles. But miracles are reserved only for the deserving.

I don't suggest depending upon miracles in this world, though we all surely believe in them I don't advise expecting them to happen, just because you wish them to.

Hezki surely knew how to be convincing. He had his audience on the edge of their seats for half an hour while relating the story of this obstinate family who would not give up their goal. But against all odd they did succeed in their quest.

Then turning to the young ladies he addressed them, "Now *haverot*, can you explain how you suddenly became rich so quickly? Maybe these young men might learn a lesson from your experiences that would help them".

Pearl began to explain, "Being a nursing assistant in the hospital by day, I took upon myself to take care of an elderly lady who lived alone and hired me to help. I spent my nights at her home and even earned a wage. As her situation deteriorated she also hired Shashana to be with her during the daytime. This arrangement was very good for us, as we had a place to sleep without paying rent. We even arranged with her to allow Rachel to share some of the chores, also allowing her to stay in her house, as well. The savings on rent may not have been so great, but it helped us put together a fair sum towards our *Alyiah* costs.

All went well for the past nine or ten months and we all had a hand in caring for this lady who literally had no living relatives.

Hezki interrupted, "That still doesn't explain your sudden windfall".

Well, yesterday she died. It was expected that she wouldn't live forever but it was still quite a shock. However she died peacefully during her afternoon nap.

Rachel was present with Shoshana at the time and not really knowing what to do; they considered changing her clothing into a fresh clean dress before calling in a doctor.

That's when they discovered an envelope tied to her thigh. It contained a letter to the three of us explicitly by our names bequeathing to all three of us all the money she had left with instructions where it would be found. Shoshana ran right to the hospital to call me, telling me that the lady just died.

We returned to the flat with a doctor who following a brief examination filled out a death certificate.

That's why no matter how weak she had been never allowed any of us to help her get dressed. She was hiding that letter.

Then we re-read the letter that instructed us to call the funeral director to make arrangements for her to be cremated. We were to pay for the service from the money she left. According to her wishes the remainder was to be distributed to the three of us.

After paying for the cremation service the balance left was just over six thousand Liras.

So that's how we became rich enough to make our *Alyiah* without further delay".

"Fascinating! Unbelievable! What a miracle! I guess some people have good luck when they need it. We'll have to work out your trip tomorrow night, after I've made some arrangements. We meet tomorrow night at exactly ten, not a minute before".

Rachel then spoke up, "What about these men, are they ready to go as well"?

"Is it really any concern of yours? asked Hezki".

With a sly smile Rachel replied, "Maybe".

CHAPTER VII

Rachel continued, "I'm not exactly comfortable about what I'm going to say and the way I'm saying it may sound odd". How odd, she hadn't anticipated, but continued; addressing Ben, "What about you Curly? Are you prepared for *Aliyah* yet"?

Ben, the only one of the five with a glorious crown of auburn colored curly hair, furtively glanced around at his friends to assure himself that it was he, to whom she directed her question, hesitatingly replied, "Not quite, but like Hezki asked, what does it mean to you"?

With apparent discomfort she continued, "If it's a matter of money, would you accept auxiliary funding to expedite your immediate *Aliyah*"?.

Turning beet red, Ben backed off with, "Thank you for your generous offer, but I'm afraid I must refuse". He had never been propositioned like that before and hardly knew how to grapple with such a situation. He couldn't comprehend why anybody, let alone a strange woman, would offer to help pay for his trip. His entire upbringing had been based on modesty, especially between the sexes.

Following a few seconds of reflection on the situation he continued, "You know nothing about me other than the color and curl of my hair. Have you any idea where I come from? What I do for a living? Or what kind of person I am. Are you not afraid that I might take unfair advantage of you? You don't even know my name. Is it not presumptuous of you to approach me, a total stranger to accept your largess? Under such circumstances, why should I trust you? Should I not suspect some ulterior motive to your proposal? Besides which, There is no way I could break off from my friends. At least till we reach *Eretz Israel* and each one of us heads towards his own destination".

The shocked silence that accompanied Ben's incredulous outburst suddenly collapsed, as everybody in the room exploded into a cacophony of cross-talk in every which direction. They had just been witness to a preposterous proposition and an explicit refusal. The offer made by this tall young lady sounded dead serious, even too serious, seeming to suggest more than just a cash subsidy, reflecting some implication much more than just a *gmeilut hessed* to a prospective *Oleh*. And his outright refusal seemed to be based upon relatively lame excuses. What an opportunity he had in hand, and he turned it down flat, without even giving himself a chance to consider the implication! Unbelievable!

Then again if such an exchange had taken place in a more subdued environment, without onlookers the entire dialogue might surely have been very much different.

Not only were Ben's buddies shocked at his retort, but Rachel's friends who had known her to be so demure till this moment could hardly believe what she was suggesting to a stranger. Her proposal seemed to imply, "Come on and join me for the voyage, I'll even pay your fare".

Rachel, who was a sensible girl, perceived the tense atmosphere that had been created by what might have been construed as an improper proposition. Blushingly she tried to reassure her audience that her intension was far from what it may have sounded.

Not knowing any of the boys' names she was just inquiring about how they were progressing with their preparations and found it easy to address such a flippant suggestion towards the one who possessed an outstanding feature, his curly hair.

"I had surreptitiously hoped that since we girls had been awarded such an unexpected windfall, we might help these young men fulfill their wishes to make *Alyiah*. Husband hunting, if that is what might my statement might have been construed to be, was far from my mind. At sixteen I'm hardly ready for that".

The other girls huddled with Rachel in order to comfort her in her moment of embarrassment, while the boys thronged together in the opposite corner to congratulate him on voicing his attitude and show of comradeship.

Within a short time the three young ladies approached Hezki to include him in their discussion. He listened intently to what they had to say, and then signaled for silence. He had an important announcement to make and wanted the undivided attention of all present.

"Hevraia", he declare, "I have some wonderful news for you. These three young women have decided to subsidize the cost of the ship fare for all of you young men till you all reach the port of Jaffo".

Fishel announced, "But we must keep in contact in order to repay our debt, otherwise I, for one, cannot accept such an offer".

Other voices concurred, "Certainly"! "Definitely"! "Without a doubt"!

Hezki reminded them once more, "We all meet here tomorrow night at ten, after I've had a chance to organize your voyage to *Eretz Israel*". So bring your passports and any other documents that might be necessary. Tomorrow night, here at ten PM.

CHAPTER VIII

Within the next few days a frenzy of activity kept the prospective *Olim* occupied with last minute preparations that would bring them to the shores of Palestine.

Arrangements were made with a freighter that might or might not load or unload cargo at some port or other along the way. Therefore the voyage might take anywhere from four days to a week. Or more. They would have to arrange for their own kosher meals and that meant depending upon Moshe's expertise in shopping for the provisions in sufficient quantities to feed all eight who would be traveling together so as not to run short.

By mid-week all was set and early on Thursday morning they all met on the quay in the Port of Haydarpasa in Constantinople, prepared to board the S/S Sadyklar, a steam driven vessel. Each one of the passengers, with his/er hand luggage, passport and ticket in hand ascended the gang-plank to the ship's deck to be greeted by a ship's officer who led them to the cabins where the heavy baggage was already awaiting their arrival.

Only Ben was carrying his heavy toolbox that he refused to entrust to the longshore-men. His father had been employed as manager of a logging operation and at a very young age Ben often accompanied him to the company forest where lumberjacks felled selected trees in order to fill specific orders. His father's decisions were based upon the size of the trunk and type of wood requisitioned by any one of the several sawmills in the area.

In summer and fall the timber was floated downstream by the swift currents of the Bahlui River a tributary of the Jijia that in turn is a tributary of the Prut. In winter the logs were moved by horses over the snow. In this way the logs could be supplied efficiently to various sawmills in the area.

Ben became intimately knowledgeable with the different kinds of trees and the qualities of the lumber that was produced by the lumber mills. Occasionally he accompanied his father on his many visits to the forestry's customers

At an early age Ben was apprenticed to a carpentry shop where delicate furniture was meticulously produced and where he became adept in the fine art of professional cabinet making. He learned how to use the proper woods and to effectively manipulate the correct tools properly in order to achieve maximum results.

One of the tests that we was obliged to perform in order to prove his skills was to design and build his own wooden tool chest, the one he was so proud of. The one he wouldn't entrust to anybody else. It not only looked valuable, it really was and contained all the important tools of his trade.

This sea voyage, being a first for them all, the curious passengers wandered throughout the vessel exploring every corner of every deck to become acquainted with their new, though temporary home.

However Moshe immediately made for the galley where he met with the ship's cook; introducing himself as having been a ship's cook in the past. He quickly made friends with the chef. Explaining, since he represented a group of passengers who adhered to a strictly kosher diet, requested permission to use the available facilities to prepare their meals for them, assuring the chef that he wouldn't disturb them in any way. Because of his tactful approach he was even offered space in the ice-box to store any perishables.

His first chore was to prepare sandwiches and coffee for his comrades, who probably hadn't yet tasted anything due to the aura of excitement that blotted out any thought of food.

Several hours passed and the ship had not yet cast off. A substantial cargo of onions was being loaded into a hold at just about the center of the ship. In conversation with an affable member of the crew they found out that their next port of call would be Limassol in Cyprus, where the load of onions would be unloaded and a different commodity waited them for transport to a different unscheduled port of call.

Finally, towards evening the ship's whistle signaled that they were preparing to head for the open sea. A powerful tug boat carefully nudged the S/S Sadyklar out of its berth and on its way through the Sea of Marmora. During the night they passed north of the Isle of Saralar heading for the narrow Dardanelles south of Gallipoli Peninsula. It was a good thing that this part of the voyage was undertaken during the day, because navigation at night would have been scary, even for experienced sea-men.

The journey was uneventful as they exited the Aegean Sea and headed in a south easterly direction through the Mediterranean Sea towards the next port of call, within the Akrotiri Bay to the port of Limassol (Lemesos) on the Island of Cyprus. This is where while the load of onions was being dropped off and a shipment of glassware was simultaneously taken on and was carefully being placed in a different hold.

Towards nightfall, the ship was once again towed into the Akrotiri Bay where she took on a westerly tack through the Mediterranean Sea towards the next port, Tartus on the East coast of Syria. Here the ship took on a load of huge bags of nuts, for delivery to Alexandria in Egypt.

During the loading and unloading of these cargos the passengers were issued temporary landing cards by the ship's purser and were usually permitted; no, not merely permitted, but encouraged to disembark and spend a few hours at each post of call. The local merchants usually profited by these short visits, as tourists are expected to spend money shopping for "bargains". However these youngsters were not in the mood for making any really unnecessary purchases. The main reason for having the travelers disembark during the loading and unloading procedures was to get them out of the way, usually for their own safety, while ropes and cables were continuously swinging to and fro with several winches working simultaneously in order to expedite the work as quickly as possible, in order to set sail with the least delay. Unnecessary time spent in a harbor could be costly.

At their next port of call, Beirut on the coast of Lebanon, another of the ship's holds was being filled with numerous bags of cement, headed for the next port, Jaffo. With the Tel Aviv building boom in full swing, this was a commodity in much demand.

Another day and a half of sailing southward brought them to *Eretz Israel*.

Jaffo was not a deep port so even before the ship dropped anchor scores of little boats headed out from the coast to surround any incoming ship, some hoping that tourists would buy their wares, others offering to ferry disembarking passengers and their baggage to dry land for a fee that usually had to be negotiated.

Prices were usually quoted and haggled between the boat-operators and their prospective customers through a cacophony of voices yelling in all manner of shouting.

This is where Ben outshone the efforts of his comrades. He collected them together and offered to be their negotiator. As they stepped back from the ship's rail pretending that they had no interest at all in disembarking, the only lone face they perceived was that of Ben. Many of the boat owners gave up and returned to dry land. As the competition trimmed down and the situation changed and Ben, who showed that that he was in no hurry, was able to convince those remaining couple of ferry service operators that it was to their benefit to agree to his offer. They grudgingly accepted and only then did the entire group of eight, begin lowering their luggage, then climbed down the ladders to the two small boats, that now seemed to loom larger than they had appeared when seen from above, from deck level.

While all this was gong on the ship was refilling its hold with a load of premium quality Hadera watermelons that were in great demand in Alexandria, especially after having won prizes for quality at the Berlin Food Fair.

CHAPTER IX

The eight new *Olim* were personally welcomed by Dr. Yehuda Leib Pinsker at the Jewish Colonization Association offices in Jaffo. He interviewed each one in order to properly direct them to the destination that matched his or her criteria best.

As Ben had perceived by himself due to his expertise that could best be exploited at the Winery in either Rehovot or, the newest one at Zichron Yaacov, who would require his skills even more, that was where he was directed. The boat along the coast to Tantura was about to shove off so he was immediately booked for the trip. Everything happened so quickly that he hadn't even been able to properly take leae of his *Heraiya*. From Tantura it was not far from Zichron Yaacov, an uphill ride by horse and wagon. He as warmly welcomed by the populace who were nearly all of Romanian origin. Upon arrival he was ceremoniously treated to a bowl of mamaliga, a cereal cooked up from corn meal, the traditional fare of his homeland.

Zichron Yaacov established at the southern tip of Mount Karmel named for Yaacov (known as James), the father of Baron Edmond de Rothschild, who himself resided in Paris. The settlement, founded in 1882 as a farming village by Romanian immigrants, was originally called Zimmarin, the name of the adjacent Arab village. The farmers struggled unsuccessfully for two years till Baron de Rothschild took upon himself to support the enterprise. He introduced viticulture as the main agricultural crop and built a huge wine cellar. However, even though he made sure that everybody was gainfully employed within the enterprise that his administrators ruled over with an iron fist.

Ben was assigned living quarters along with a few other bachelors. Upon completing his interview at the winery he was accepted on a trial basis as a cooper. He worked under the tutelage of a master cooper and quickly proved his skills, as he had already spent a year learning the basics, making wooden kegs while still in his native land.

He was paid, what was considered, a fair wage and began saving money in order to repay the girls for their "loan".

Ben made friends easily and advanced with his work. He was entrusted with repairing the wooden barrels that came in all sizes. Maintenance was not the most flattering job in the coopery, but in reality required more skill than manufacturing new wooden casks. With old kegs the dilemma required proficiency in identifying the problems and rectifying them effectively. In that realm, Ben excelled.

However he had a problem. As he was the first one to be shipped out of Jaffo to this destination so quickly he hadn't been able to find out how to make contact with his benefactors in order to repay them. In fact he was totally ignorant of where any of the rest of the group had ended up. He still had hopes of eventually finding them, but it still irked him that he didn't even know the family names of any of the three young women, adding to the difficulty in locating any of them. He realized that if too much time passed and when any of them would marry, the difficulty in locating would be compounded following a probable name change.

However the Almighty has his ways in manipulating His world . . .

With nothing much else to do during the evening hours and as the bachelors didn't have families to keep them busy they told and retold stories about events that were considered interesting or even entertaining.

Local legend had it that one of the setters had ridden out of town on his horse and was delayed in returning before nightfall. The sky became overcast with thick low clouds. No moon at all and visibility was zero. He very quickly lost the trail and because it had been pouring for the past few days the cascading waters had cut innumerable gullies in every which way across the fields. It was a menacing situation, and with the heavily laden clouds overhead threatening a fresh deluge that could have begun at any moment. He was completely lost, but has one hope. He had confidence in his mare that she would find a safe way home.

Releasing the reigns and putting his trust in the animal instincts of his beast, while whispering prayers to the Creator, his mount slowly made her way this way and that. She sometimes stopped and sidestepped some dangerous spot, sometimes pawing the ground then changing tack, but still moving forward. Eventually signs of habitation shone through the murky darkness, as they approached a house on the edge of the village that still showed light emanating from a kerosene lantern.

He heard other stories concerned events that didn't directly affect local townspeople, but some of the neighboring towns as well. A humorous episode had happened quite a few years in the past. A young man from Hadera had come to the winery to buy a bottle of wine, Proudly proclaiming that he was about to take a wife on the morrow, actually the first wedding to take place in the settlement since the founding of Hadera. Early next morning he returned to buy another.

"What happened"? One local asked, "Did the bottle break"? Another, in jest, "Are you taking a second wife already"? Workers at the winery always had a humorous bent.

He seriously explained that when he got home he hid the wine under his bed, but someone found it. Towards evening his friends invited him, the groom, to a bachelor party. He couldn't very well refuse and they all had a good time sipping wine and partaking of goodies. Upon returning to his room he discovered, it had been his own wine they all shared. Therefore, here he is again for another bottle for the wedding ceremony.

Another story that was not humorous at all concerned a fellow Romanian who lived in Hadera. Always one to take the opportunity when it was available, so that he could enjoy a bowl of authentic mamaliga, he often volunteered to make the trip to Zichron Yaacov where the regional bakery was situated, to bring back bread for the inhabitants of Hadera. On one such trip before he could return with the bread a torrential rain had begun, making the return trip too hazardous to attempt. However men women and children would be deprived of their daily bread if they didn't get the shipment. They didn't call him the "Zany Romanian" for nothing, but he was not entirely out of his mind. He wrapped up the shipment well, tied it to his horse with a note that he was staying over in Zichron Yaacov till the road would be safe, and sent his horse with its load on its own, to return to Hadera.

Darkness had already fallen and the residents were very much concerned about the "Zany Romanian" who hadn't returned. They wondered if something drastic had not happened to him in this blustery weather, till someone heard the sound of horse hoofs splashing in the mud. When they made out that the horse had arrived without its rider they were really worried till someone found the letter letting them know that he was safely spending the time with his friends.

Shortly after that episode a local builder constructed a proper oven so that Haderaites would not be dependent on the Zichron Yaacov bakery for their daily bread.

Such were the kind of stories that were told and retold, sometimes even embellished a bit so as not become boring.

A few years had passed uneventfully while Ben saved his spare cash. He was confident that he would somehow locate at least one of those three goodhearted women who helped him in his hour of need.

However the Almighty has his ways of manipulating His world . . .

CHAPTER X

One of the bachelors cheerfully announced that he found the right girl and was getting married. Naturally the inhabitants of the entire town were glad. But none were more pleased that the other bachelors. Now there would less competition in finding a suitable mate, if and when any girls would arrive on the scene. And a wedding usually brought guests. Among them would surely be some eligible young women. That probably caused more joy among the unattached males than the actual wedding itself.

Ben still found himself hoping to find at least one of the three among the invited guests who had made *Alyiah* with him.

The date of the wedding had finally arrived, and with it a great number of guests from all over the country. Some came from Jerusalem, others from Jaffo and the new city of Tel Aviv. But most, from the near-by settlement, Hadera, whose members were always looking foreword to celebrate joyous occasions with their friends and neighbors.

As the horse-drawn wagons began arriving local residents made it their business to greet the passengers, inviting them into their homes to revive them and partake of some refreshments following the tedious trip that some had made over long distances. The locals really knew how to entertain guests, even if they were complete strangers.

As dusk was approaching the town square was beginning to fill up, as people made their way from every which direction towards the bridal canopy that was already tightly stretched on four poles over a platform made up of wooden boxes covered by a smooth clean canvas sheet.

Everybody was milling about, some greeting acquaintances; others making friends while still others were just wandering around observing the latest styles that were being worn to such occasions. However most of the women were waiting in the procession wishing to get a glimpse of the bride. After all she was about to become a local resident.

It was then that Ben caught sight of Pearl and made his way towards her, not really sure how to open the conversation. She solved that problem when she recognized him just as he was approaching.

"Shalom Ben! I was hoping to meet you some day. You left Jaffo so suddenly on the day we arrived that we couldn't let you know what happened with us".

"Well I myself was taken by surprise when told that a boat was leaving to Tantura and if I missed that opportunity I'd have to hang around for another week. It was completely out of my control. What are you doing with yourself"?

"Do you remember that I had trained to be a nurse? Well I was offered to join the nursing staff at the Jaffo Hospital and am still there, but not as a helper any more. I'm responsible for an entire department now".

"That's great. But how do you relate to this celebration"?

"Let me begin with the reason I'm here. The bride, Miriam is a registered nurse. She was in charge of the department in the Jaffo Hospital. In fact, I'm taking over the responsibility that had been hers till she quit to get married. After she ends the week of *Sheva Brachot* she'll be working in Dr. Hillel Joffe's hospital right here in town. Isn't that great? Now you know why I'm here. I'm so thrilled that I was asked to be the bride's "Maid-of-honor"! And I'm familiar enough with Miriam to know that she'll be a perfect wife for your fried Baruch".

"You don't realize how happy I am that you're here. I have a debt to repay to you and your friends".

"You don't owe me a thing. Your fare was fully covered by Rachel. Didn't you realize that she had a crush on you"?

"That entire scene was very unnerving, both for her as well as for me. I'm sorry if she felt hurt in any way by my reaction, but the whole thing was so unexpected. If I knew how to get in contact with her I'd apologize for reacting in such an immature manner".

"Oh, go on. You were perfect. It was she who overstepped the boundary of good taste, given the situation. In fact, did you ever visit your neighboring village, Hadera"?

"No. I'm must admit that since the day I arrived in Zichron I never left the place, and that's nearly four years. Maybe I should get out for a change of scenery. You're right about that. But why did you specifically mention Hadera? Aren't there ant other more interesting places to visit"?

"Oh, Ben. When are you going begin to understand what I'm driving at? Hadera is not just a village. That is where your true love awaits you! Rachel is the kindergarten teacher in Hadera. That's why she's not here now. So many people left to attend this wedding, and because she was free and big-hearted, she volunteered to stay behind and keep an eye on their children".

"You're kidding. You mean to tell me that Rachel has been living such a short distance from here all this time? I can't believe it! I'm such an idiot! Pearl, please tell me you're not joking".

"Ben, how can I spell it out any clearer? Rachel lives in Hadera, and has been, since the day after making *Alyiah*. Nearly four years already".

The very next day Ben dressed in his best, borrowed a horse and rode off towards Hadera. The road was not straight but took advantage of what nature had carved out of the contours that the wind and rain had formed over the years. The sun had not yet reached its zenith when he approached. He saw rows of huge eucalyptus trees in the distance, for which Hadera was widely known and knew that his goal was straight ahead.

Slowing his mount to a trot then as he drew closer to the entrance further reduced his sped to a saunter.

Approaching the main gate gave him a thrill that he hadn't felt for many years. Within a short time he would be in the company of the girl that had been on his mind without really seriously believing that he would ever meet her again.

Dismounting in reverence to the anticipated occasion he led his horse on foot along the main thoroughfare till he met someone to to inquire . . . .

"Pardon me, would you please tell me where I can find the kindergarten teacher"?

"Oh, you must mean Rachel. Sure. If you continue straight along, past the fourth house and turn right you'll see the small park with a miniature house. That's the kindergarten area. She'll be there".

With a smile and a "Thank you" he continued on his way, slowing down still more in order to plan his opening words. Excitement welled up in his breast and his head seemed to be in the clouds at the thought of the forthcoming meeting with this young girl who had taken a liking to him even before he realized what might have been behind her shy but not timid proposal some four years ago. Passing four freshly built homes he caught sight of the diminutive house just some fifty meters or so from where he stood, but hadn't seen anybody. Making his way towards what was supposed to be the kindergarten he heard childish voices singing but hadn't yet caught sight of them till he passed the little cabin that was built on a slight rise, hiding them from view. There were some twenty little boys and girls sitting in a complete circle with their teacher standing in the center. She happened to be facing in the other direction so didn't perceive his approach. Some of the tots noticed Ben leading his horse causing some of the singing to falter, their eyes turned in his direction. It didn't take more than a few seconds before all the little faces turned to observe the approaching stranger dressed in his finery. When the singing stopped altogether Rachel turned to see what caused the disturbance. It took her a few seconds to realize who that stranger was. She had to restrain herself from leaving her charges to run and greet the tall well dressed gentlemen who had just showed up without prior warning still sporting a thin veil of dust from the trip.

She called to her assistant who was in the kindergarten dining room getting together the mid-morning snack, "Tova, please come out and take over the activity". Proving that her responsibility to her charges came first, no matter what, she awaited the approach of Tova before taking leave of the children to greet her visitor.

CHAPTER XI

"Ben, Ben. So you finally showed up. What took you so long"?

"Rachel, I really don't know how to explain but only last night did I find out that you're here, when Pearl attended a wedding in Zichron Yaacov. Till then I had no idea how to find you. I still have a debt to repay you for your kindness".

"Is that the only thing on your mind? It's only a paltry sum that I'd already forgotten about long ago. Is that all that you worry about, Ben—only the money"?

"Rachel, I'm really not adept at this kind of thing, but yes, I did think about you, about us. I really wished to find you but had no idea how to begin. I've been living in, Zichron Yaacov since the day I arrived there and have been busy at the coopery, even spending extra time on the job in order to keep my mind occupied. But yes, I did think abut you a lot. Can we see each other more often"?

"Yes Ben, yes. Certainly we can see each other regularly. It's not easy for me to travel the roads alone, but come on over as often as you can. I'd like that very much"

"But I must repay you for the *Hessed* that you performed". Reaching into his pouch he withdrew a thick wallet and continued, "I have it right here with me. Please accept my apologies for having taken so long to repay you. The way I'd been brought up it's crucial for a borrower to repay any debt as soon as possible. I cannot abide by delaying it even for another day".

"Ben dear, actually this not the place or the time to go into details, but I don't want it at this time. However I would accept it at a later date with a condition. And that is, if you present it to me as a gift of betrothal, but not until I'm prepared for that".

Ben was taken aback at that suggestion. Was this an outright proposal of marriage? If he refused to such an arrangement and she wouldn't accept the cash he would be forever indebted to her. How could he live with himself under such circumstances?

"I—I'll have to think about what you suggest. This is not something I can decide at the moment. We really hardly know each other and that would be a lifetime commitment".

"If we meet more frequently I'm sure we'll get to know more about each other and even find that we might even have many interests in common. I realize that we have a lot of ground to cover but let's give ourselves time. Meanwhile hold onto that money it has a very special value. You don't yet realize how much, so don't squander it yet"

"So is that the note that I am to leave on? That we carry on discussions before you'll accept what is really yours? I've never heard of such a situation. Where did you ever dream up such an idea? Who ever thought to make repayment of a loan a betrothal gift"?

Then with a devious smile on his face added, "You sure have a devious mind; however I'll give it some serious thought".

"Ben you look troubled about my conditions, but please don't leave yet. I'd like to invite you for lunch without discussing serious matters. I can have it ready in ten minutes. Meanwhile you can observe the children and how they play some educational and dextral games that I developed for them".

Ben watered his horse, gave him a handful of oats and sat down with her to a meal of scrambled eggs with a fresh vegetable salad, followed by freshly grilled fish that had been gown in the local fish ponds.

"Please confirm a few things that have been recounted as folk tales. Was there ever such a person living here in Hadera, known as the "Zany Romanian"?

"Sure he was a hero here in town. That was Reuven Bilinki. He died a very short time after having arrived in Hadera, but there are some mix ups with the records. Some believet that he died in Jaffo. Probably at the hospital, as many locals were treated for Malaria there in the early days. It was also reported that his bones were brought back to Hadera for burial. But to complicate matters he's registered in the records of the *Hevra Kadisha* in Zichron Yaacov as being buried there on the fist of *Elul* 1893".

"There's still a mystery to the whole thing. If he was a resident of Hadera and died in Jaffo, why would he be buried in Zichron, unless he died in the hospital in Zichron Yaacov and was interred there".

"Is it possible, thought that because he originally came from Romania it might have been decided to bury him among other Romanians"?

"Lots of theories have been considered but still no one knows for sure".

"So the story about his sending bread with a rider-less horse is true"?

"It certainly is, according to all the residents of that time".

"After this fine lunch, would you be free to show me the oven that was erected a result of that episode"?

"So that's the famous oven that Schektzer built. I can now verify that I actually saw the oven.

"About this Reuven Bilinki, can't the mystery be solved by locating his grave? Is it in Hadera or in Zichron Yaacov"?

"That was attempted by many, but it seems that no monument was ever found and his place of interment is still uncertain. That is one of the tragedies of having lived and died without any family to attend to those details".

"Rachel, I wish to thank you for your hospitality and am happy that you bear me no grudge for not finding you earlier. I'll give some serious consideration to your proposal, even though I think of it as outrageous. One way or another I promise to visit frequently. After all we have a lot to catch up on. So Goodbye, *Lehitraot*".

He unfettered his horse and led him out to the main road before mounting and riding back to Zichron Yaacov with bewildered thoughts milling though his mind. What a strange woman! Smart? Crafty? Cunning? Clever? He couldn't place her in any specific category, but she might fit any of them or a combination of all. What a woman!

CHAPTER XII

During the return trip he was trying to consider who would be the best person to approach for advice about how to handle his problem with Rachel.

He knew that he couldn't confide in anybody in Zichron. Anything he would say might be construed as *lashon hara* (malicious gossip). Even the Rabbi might not comprehend that the Rachel's strategy was not in any way spiteful. It was just her way of straightforwardly expressing her aspiration.

Pearl was the only one he could turn to. She was well acquainted with Rachel. Boy how that woman could formulate such a foolproof scheme that would control him one way or another, not allowing him any way to avoid entrapment.

As soon as Ben got to Zichron Yaacov he returned the horse to its owner, not wishing to spoil his chances of borrowing the horse when he'd need it again. Thereafter he immediately signed up for space on the next trip of the horse-drawn transport, called a "diligence" (an inter-town horse car) that would get him to Jaffo.

He had offhandedly remarked to his supervisor at the coopery that he would need some vacation time at a moment's open notice during the next few days, not yet certain when it would take effect. Two days later he was informed that the "diligence" would be coming through Zichron Yaacov shortly and he made certain to be at the station on time.

The trip via Tul Karem and Petah Tiqva took nearly a whole day. Even though dusk was falling when they reached the final stop he made his way directly to the Jaffo Hospital.

He was directed to the infirmary where a lamp was already lit to ward off the growing darkness and easily identified her by her starched white nurse's uniform.

Not wishing to startle he quietly called out to her, "Pearl".

"Oh Ben, I had no idea we'd be seeing each other so soon. Did you get to speak to Rachel yet"?

"Yes I did get to see her. On the very next morning after we met I borrowed a horse and rode to Hadera. Finding her was easy, as she works in the village and not out in the fields.

Are you busy right now"?

"No. I'm on a late afternoon break till eight o'clock, so we have plenty of time to talk. Oh, how impolite of me not to offer you some tea. You must also be awfully hungry after such a long journey. Can I offer you something to eat"?

"Thank you but tea will be just right. I located her quite easily. Thanks a million for telling me about where I could find her. And that's why I'm here right now. I have a serious problem and don't know to whom I can turn to other that to you in order to solve it".

"You hardly had time to become re-acquainted and already you have a serious problem serious enough to bring you all the way to Jaffo"?

Ben didn't want to sound like a whiner, or still worse, a gossip. He couldn't accuse Rachel of anything underhanded. She hadn't done anything deceitful. He had to carefully choose his words. How could he state his case yet not place any blame on Rachel. After all she didn't cause any harm with her strategic trap. He was still free to choose his destiny. She was not [yet] twisting his arm, in any physical sense. That's what bothered him. He had a compliant to make, but nothing had happened. He still owed her a large sum of money and he was still in possession of it. She was not pressing for it, yet didn't want to accept it till she would decide when to call in her voluntary loan. She hadn't had any lien on him. There were no guarantors involved who could be affected. Yet she was dictating the terms. That matter of "not yet" had perturbed him. How was he supposed to explain to Pearl how such a sensitive situation could really offend his righteous attitude toward repaying a debt outright with no strings attached? How could he escape the quagmire that was sucking him into an inescapable situation?

"Ben! Ben! Snap out of it. Did you travel all day just to sit and stare at a glass of cold tea and mutter to yourself? Is that why you came all this distance to see me? Come on and tell me what's on your mind. I can't guarantee that I can assist you. But if you don't tell me, I definitely can't be of any help".

"I don't really know how to explain. It's a situation that doesn't exist so how can I describe it. It's not a threat, but is on the threshold of being one".

"Then why not start at the beginning? Take one step at a time. You seemed so happy at the idea of meeting Rachel, so you borrowed a horse and rode off to meet her. You found her and spoke to her. What happened that finds you in such a pensive mood? Was it something you saw? Something you said? Something she said? During that short visit, it couldn't have been anything else. Or am I wrong? I know Rachel and am well aware that she can often utter a word that might be construed in the wrong context. So what did you discuss that might have brought about such a critical dilemma that brings you all the way to Jaffo? Ben, pretend I'm an older sister who would listen and advise you how to escape from the predicament you perceive that you find yourself in. You seem to be tied into knots and need someone to help untangle them for you. Come-on and just tell me".

"It's the debt that I owe her. I must have been awfully naïve when I accepted the loan back then in Turkey. But as with a piece of glass that is backed with silver, one does not perceive what lies ahead, and I was blinded by the gesture. I never imagined that I could find myself in such a dismal state of affairs. Is it not normal for a creditor to wholeheartedly accept repayment of a loan? Well then Rachel is not that kind. She refuses to accept it, except under her conditions. Meanwhile here I am a debtor who just wishes to rid myself of the obligation as soon as possible, but she won't have it. She just refuses to take it".

"Did she tell you to keep it"?

"No".

"Did she say to forget it altogether"?

"No".

"So what did she actually say that so disturbs you? It surely must be something awful".

"I really find it hard to believe, never mind to repeat it. She said that sometime in the future, when she's ready, she'll accept the money if I offer it to her as a gift of betrothal. Am I correct in assuming that means she won't accept repayment of the loan if I don't marry her"?

"What!! Did she actually come out and say that in those words? I guess she just might have done so, especially since she first laid eyes upon you that night in the meeting hall. Yes. That's just like her. What a devious way to get a husband! I guess that's Rachel. She's outspoken but she's shrewd".

"You can say that again. She sure is a shrew".

"No Ben. She's shrewd, but definitely not a shrew. Though she may be a conniver she's not a shrew. She would never harm anybody, especially you. But then again Ben you're not getting any younger and she actually could be a good wife".

"Pearl, are you advising me to marry a woman with such a devious mind? I can't believe that you're even suggesting I accept her terms? This is not some parlor game that is over in an hour or two. Marriage is for a lifetime and I'd have to be on my toes every moment to be sure I'm not being manipulated into something that I might regret".

"Actually Ben, at least you know that Rachel is straight. Her heart and her mouth are of one accord. She is not devious in the way you perceive and neither is she a cheater. Four years ago she made up her mind and didn't stray even one iota from her plan. She just patiently awaited the opportunity and finally you found the way to help her achieve her goal".

"I? What did I do to invite such a situation"?

"You insist on repaying her loan. Yes, you are the one causing your own quandary".

She has always wanted to be Mrs. Hershcu, and, with your cooperation she shall be, the loving wife of Ben Hershcu".

"Pearl, this is not what I expected when I came to you for advice. But your "sisterly" counsel gives my something to consider. It will definitely take some time for me to absorb the idea, but I promise that I'll consider it before making any decisions that I might regret. Another thing, Pearl, do you by any chance have any information on the other members of our *Alyiah* group"?

"Yes Ben, and you're going to need their addresses when you send out the wedding invitations. I'll send you the list by tomorrow's post".

CHAPTER XIII

Ben had the good fortune to book passage on the last seat of the return trip of the horse drawn diligence. Throughout the entire trip he had much time to ponder what lay ahead of him. He had all day to think. How was he to yield to Rachel's scheme and yet show that he is the one determining their fate? It was not a simple step to take. At present she had the upper hand and he was on the defensive. He wouldn't be comfortable if she was the victor of their struggle. She held all the cards but one. He only had the cash. How could he take the initiative? There must be a bright spot behind the tight spot wherein he found himself. During the many hours of the trip Ben's brain worked in overdrive, considering every angle that came to mind.

After passing through Tul Karem, he couldn't stay awake any longer and fell asleep. It's not often that one dreams during a short daytime nap, as there is hardly any time to really develop a deep enough sleep for the subconscious mind to become active enough to produce a dream. However Ben was so fatigued, and the fact that his brain was still attempting to solve his problem that he did have a revelation.

He was gently aroused by one of the passengers as they approached Zichron Yaacov. This was his destination and it was time to alight. However an idea how to tackle the problem had formulated during that nap.

His final conclusion was that if he couldn't repay his debt he wouldn't be able to live with himself. If he wouldn't live with himself he may as well be resigned to the fact that he'd have to live with someone else. So it may as well be with Rachel after all.

Realizing that he had little choice he had to play the game smoothly and in a natural way. For the next several months he would visit Rachel in Hadera frequently, occasionally bearing small gifts as was expected of a normal suitor seriously dating the one he desires. He was going to have to intersperse his dates with letters sincerely expressing his feeling for her, till the time seemed right to propose marriage.

She would be expecting such an approach anyway, but he must first convince himself that he was the prime mover and gain self-confidence that he really was taking the initiative. Only then could he readily persuade her that he was in charge.

It was a foregone conclusion that he was going to take her for a wife anyway so why fight it. His best approach was that he fully accept his fate, such is destiny.

There is nothing like a little relaxing sleep to solve a problem that otherwise seems too complex to handle while awake.

However he found a loophole in her plan and had every intension of exploiting it. Yes he would take her for a wife.

Shortly after having made up his mind to pursue his intentions earnestly he paid another visit to his girl in Hadera, this time in the late afternoon so as not to disturb her during working hours. This was possible because at that time of year the hours of daylight were growing longer. He found their time together to be quite interesting as she proved to be well read, witty and possessing a sense of humor. Even though they could spend a bit more time in each other's company during each visit as the days grew longer Ben searched out and found several short-cuts that he could safely maneuver with his horse, thus increasing the time that they spent together.

This was beginning to develop into a serious relationship and Ben found himself courting Rachel in earnest. He sought out various little gifts that surprised her each time he called on her.

The summer months passed their zenith and the longest days of the year were beginning to surrender to the change in nature. Ben found that he had to cut his visits shorter each time in order to return home before darkness would totally obliterate the paths that he must navigate safely.

Tu B'av, the 15th of the month of Av was fast approaching. It is one of the lesser-known days on the Jewish calendar, and its focus is on the ever-popular subject, romance.

According to the *Talmud* "There were no more joyous days in the year that *Tu'BAv* and *Yom Kippur*. Those were the days when young women would borrow white clothing so no one would stand out by their wealth and dance in the vineyards. Boys would watch with a hopeful eye and anticipate being singled out by one of the girls. The *Talmud* advises the young men to choose wisely and not focus only on a woman's physical charm, but on her overall virtues. The Talmud (in *Ta'anit* 31a) states the, "Vanity is false, and physical beauty is meaningless, [but] a G-d-fearing woman is to be praised". These two days in the year permitted an eligible young woman to show interest in the particular young man who she favored.

And that is exactly what Rachel did. This time she had prepared to present Ben with a gift of her own making. On a primitive loom that she had assembled by herself, she wove a colorfully ornate *Tallit* (Prayer shawl). She had one of her neighbors string *Tzitzit* properly on each of the four corners so that it would be strictly kosher. This four cornered garment is worn by married men during prayers and at special religious functions.

Ben's next visit coincided exactly with the day of *Tu B'av*, the perfect opportunity for her to present him with the work of her own hands, the *Tallit* that she had been working on in secret for several weeks. Upon unwrapping her present he was overcome with emotion, realizing that here was the sign. The moment had arrived for him to propose marriage. As soon as he regained his composure that is exactly what he did. With a tear sparkling in his eye he took her hand in his and asked her outright, "Will you marry me"? Of course her immediate reply was in the affirmative even though he was not prepared with a ring or other suitable offering. All that remained now was to decide upon an appropriate date and venue. However that was put off for the next visit, when they would both be in a more rational state of mind.

Their next meeting found them both in an entirely different mood that had ever been till now. They discussed plans that had never yet been considered, but most important of all she agreed that the nuptials would take place in Zichron Yaacov where they would set up their household. That was where the main source of their financial base was already established.

As for the date, that was up to her and she suggested that it take place before *Rosh Hashana*. (The Jewish new year), to which Ben readily agreed. That would allow him time to locate a suitable dwelling. He'd spruce it up and furnish it with time to spare.

When it came to decide colors of the curtains as they discussed their new home and how they would decorate it, was when it was revealed that Ben was color-blind, a condition that he'd never realized before. How did that discovery come about? When Rachel mentioned different shades he spoke of hues that might resemble different foodstuffs. For instance when she mentioned yellow he asked, "You mean like bananas or like butter"? In that way she discovered that he couldn't recognize colors. But that didn't stand in the way of their decision to marry. And they did, right on schedule.

Plans were laid, invitations mailed out. Moshe arrived two days before the great event offering to organize a feast that would not be forgotten for a long time, that included a beautifully decorated four-tier wedding cake, the likes of which hadn't yet been seen in Zichron Yaacov.

CHAPTER XIV

Neither Ben nor Rachel had any relatives living in the Land of Israel but had made a good number of friends who honored the couple with their presence at their *Simcha*. The reunion of their *Garin Alyiah* was nearly as emotional as the wedding itself.

Ben was let to the platform over which was the canopy was stretched out. Rachel accompanied by her friends sang and danced all the way to the wedding canopy where she was greeted by her groom, Ben who was gleaming with joy. She performed the traditional walk around her groom seven times, before taking up her position to his right

Then with a full cup of the best wine available the Rabbi intoned the prayers that precede the actual act of betrothal, when Ben whipped out a golden wedding band, presenting it to his beloved bride while announcing, "With this ring I hereby betroth you according to the laws of Moshe and Israel"! He then slipped the ring onto the forefinger of her right hand in the presence of two witnesses, to the applause of all those in attendance.

Ben, holding up a heavy exquisitely tooled leather purse, made an announcement, "I wish to make a public declaration before reading of the *Ketuba*. In the presence of this entire assembly, I hereby explicitly declare, with the transfer of this purse to my wife, I am hereby repaying a long outstanding debt to her". And handed over the large sum that he'd been trying to return to her, but now did it on his own terms, after the betrothal, as she had already accepted the gold wedding ring.

Rachel was somewhat in shock, as she realized that she'd been bested by having the loan repaid after the actual betrothal and not as part of it the way she'd originally planed.

Ben donned his new *Taliiit,* pronounced the *Shecheyanu* blessing and wrapped it round both of them, a sign that they were now a single family unit.

The *Ketuba* outlining the commitment that a husband is obliged to carry out towards his wife was publicly recited and a glass was shattered under the groom's heel, signaling conclusion of the ceremony.

During the festivities Ben and Rachel slipped out of the wedding party to their new home.

Within a year they were fondling a son, Reuven. As the years passed three more children were born to them.

The First World War was declared and the Jews were caught up in a bitter conflict between the Ottoman Empire, who ruled the Land of Israel and the British Army. They were in a quandary as to where their interests lie. Life under the Ottoman Empire regime was harsh and it was hoped by many Jews that the British would emerge victorious. It just happened to be that the people of Zichron Yaacov were politically involved in the struggle, and became the focal point of the NILI underground organization spying against the Turks. Members of NILI were being haunted by the Turkish army and normal life was curtailed to a great extent.

Naturally Ben, who was involved in these underground activities was forced to change his name if he was to survive the witch hunt, and changed to Tzvi, a translation of Hershcu. From now on he was Ben Tzvi.

The children grew up, were well educated and raised to be devoted to their heritage.

Reuven married and in turn raised a family of six children, the first born, named Dror.

In turn Dror Ben Tzvi married and his wife presented him with three children, two of them were a set of twin daughters.

"I, Dan, am that single son, the youngest of my siblings and reside in Zichron Yaacov".

"That still doesn't explain how you located me. Can you put some light on that"?

"Oh, Shmuel that was simple. On one of my visits to the *Beit Hatifutzzot* in Ramat Gan, I entered my name in their vast computerized data bank and couldn't find it there. So I went back several generations and found my great-great grandfather, Alter and his wife, my great-great-grandmother,

Sarah Dina. When I sought out their children this is what came up: Their children were listed as:

BenZion	Hersh-Ber	Frima	Miriam	Gittel	Son	Hayia Riva
Born 28/04/1874 Romania Married **Mindel** 1898	Born Romania Married **Malka**				Probably born In 1887 (stayed in Europe)	Married **Moshe** Sakaju Their daughter **Raisel** Married **Michael** Greenberg Then **BenZion** 18/05/1953 In Bnei Brak
then **Raisel** 18/05/1953 in Bnei Brak						

"That was a nice bit of research on your part but how did you find me"?

"Shmuel, don't you realize that the family tree that I located there was the one you submitted. I just had to follow the descendents:

Ben Zion—Hayim Shimshon—Shmuel . . . and found you there". They even supplied me with your name and information how to get in touch with you". So here I am.

BECOMING JEWISH

Thunkrashhhh!! "Oh, Drat!! There goes another one, she said incoherently, under her breath, hoping nobody noticed."

But the shattering crash was overheard, as Bella's favorite mug hit the ceramic tiled floor and smashed into smithereens. "What's the matter? Can't you hold onto a cup?" came the annoyed voice from the living room.

Continuing her muttering, "Well it's time to either get a rubber mat or a plastic cup. But, yuck! Turkish coffee tastes dreadful out of plastic."

Bella entered the kitchen, where she caught Willdo still sweeping up the evidence. As matron of the house she asked, "What's troubling you?" then softening her tome, continued in a more subdued voice "You don't seem to function as you used to?"

"I, I, I guess I'm nervous", was the timid reply.

Drinking all that coffee is only making you more nervous. Then in a more tender tone continued, "You can confide in me Willdo. After all aren't you like a daughter to me? Come on, what's troubling you?"

Klanggg!

"What was that?" She asked in a panic. "You can't seem to hold onto anything anymore. Then, in a more gentle voice she continued. "Come on. After all the time we were together you can surely open your heart to me."

"It was only a spoon, and it fell into the sink. Then turning around to face Bella, she continued, "Don't worry so much. You seem to be nervous about every little sound."

"Well that was two cups in the past two days, and I'm not used to that much damage happening in my house."

"**Oh!** Yesterday? It was only the ear of an old cup that chipped off. No great harm done. And about the one that broke this morning I noticed that it was developing a crack and wasn't in the best of shape anyway."

"**Willdo,** you must do something to relax. Maybe a few days of vacation will help."

"**It's** not that. The problem is that I'm worried about my working status. My not being Jewish and all that. I want so much to convert but could find myself being deported before achieving my dying wish. And that would be a disaster. You know how much I want to live as a Jew, but all my attempts fall on deaf ears. I've tried just about every organization I could think of; including the Health and Welfare, National Insurance, Wizo, Shil and Emuna. But I couldn't find a sympathetic soul willing to help me anywhere."

"**Have** you contacted the Rabbinate? That is supposed to be in their domain."

"**They** were the first ones I approached, but they were the most unsympathetic of all. Before I even formulated my request, I was nearly thrown out of the building."

"**I'll** try to find a clever Talmudic student. Not necessarily one with a rabbinical title, but someone who is well versed in the legal intricacies of becoming an acceptable convert. Meanwhile try to pull yourself together. Your work permit is still in force for quite some time yet."

A few days later, after Bella had contacted a few of her friends she found just the man who would guide Willdo through the details of becoming a Jewess.

Raphael paid a visit to the Blum household after calling first to make sure Willdo would be at home. He showed up at exactly the preappointed time bearing a heavy tome, "On being a Jew" printed in English that he left with Willdo so she could study it towards their next meeting.

Then he got right down to the issue at hand and asked Willdo, "Would you please tell me why you find it so compelling to become Jewish. Of course, you are well aware that life as a Jew can be quite difficult, and is definitely not a pleasure.

Willdo leaned forward and placed both elbows on the glass topped walnut coffee table that stood between them. After a short pause in order to organize her thoughts she began, "I was born and raised in a very strict Christian environment. As a toddler I had been enrolled in the local missionary school, where we were instructed to believe everything that we were taught, without any doubt. And questioning anything was unacceptable. Following several years of praying by rote, and as we progressed to a ore advanced educational level we were taught to read and write, Eventually each one of us was provided with a personal new Bible. I loved to read anything that came my way and was thrilled with my new acquisition. Being the proud owner of my very own book, I spent every moment perusing every word of each page passionately. As I read through the many pages innumerable questions arose in my mind, but had nobody to confide in, as probing into anything about religion was out-of-the-question. When I read my way through the second half of the book, the New Testament, I found so many inconsistencies that I was in a complete turmoil. It was only when I re-read the beginning of the Bible, the Old Testament that I began to understand that there was something special about the Jewish religion. It's authentically original and not a false copy of the real thing. But I still had nobody to discuss my thoughts with.

For a few years after graduating from school I worked at various jobs. I had been filing letters, selling shoes, cashiering in a food store, helping at a kindergarten, and even aiding a seamstress for a few months. During this time I was able to contribute part of my earnings to my parents and managed to save some money, as well.

"In time I found out about the land of Israel that was so frequently mentioned in the Bible as being genuine.

"Somehow, word got around that workers were being sought in my country to work in Israel. When I found out that the possibility existed to actually come to Israel to work here, I sought out some way of realizing that wish and made application to join a group who would be flown here to work. My parents eventually, though grudgingly, agreed to my plea to leave, in anticipation of lots of money that would help support them. I had already passed my eighteenth birthday and was legally allowed to make my own decisions. Still in difference to my parents I still owed them the honor, as outlined in the Bible, of requesting their permission to leave them for my trip to such a far away land.

"**For** as many years as I can remember I secretly longed to join the Children of Israel as a full and active member and live as a Jew in their land. My being accepted to join the Israeli work force was a sign from heaven that my most fervent wish was also in accord with G-d's plan for my future.

"**My** ending up in the home of Bella, was further proof that my wish was being directed by G-d himself. Here, I found myself in a household where every movement was in accord with the laws as set forth in the Bible. I found that the rules about keeping a kosher home were being strictly adhered to. Shabbat and Festivals were anticipated and kept in accord with the stringencies advocated in the Torah. I had been directed to the right place.

"**But** the one thing that was missing was my not being officially accepted as a practicing Jew. I would not be allowed to marry a Jewish man when the time would prove to be right and would give anything to pass that hurdle.

"**Why** is everyone so hostile towards me when I bring up the subject? Is the Jewish nation so exclusive? Or is something wrong with me? What can I do in order to be accepted? There must surely be a solution to my problem. Mr. Raphael, Bella feels that you can find that solution. Believing that it is G-d's will, I ardently hope you can find a way for me to be legally accepted to join the fold. Bella has a lot of faith in your vast knowledge on the subject. And I hope she's right. I think I've opened my heart to you with full trust that you can help me. If there are any other questions or have I left out some important facts, please feel free to ask me.

Raphael's scribbling filled a couple of sheets with notes during Willdo's lengthy speech and he promised to study the issue, based on availability of the Talmudic and Halachic material on the subject. He promised that he'd keep in touch within the next couple of days, and with a confident air he took his leave . . .

But not before he explained, "There are several ways one becomes Jewish. The simplest one is to be born to a Jewish mother. The next one is somewhat more complicated, and that is by authorized conversion. There is still another way, but though it is much more intricate, is more binding than conversion though a rabbinical court.

"But before we go into any more details, I must check my sources, so as to be sure I have it all right." So wishing Willdo and Bella a good night, he took his leave till their next meeting.

Willdo's continence improved very much following the confidence building session that she experienced with Raphael, but awaited his next communication with impatience that she'd never experienced before.

Raphael was as good as his word, and following a phone call to ascertain that Willdo was available for further discussion, he arrived at the appointed time. She liked his promptness about keeping an appointment. This next session was conducted only between the two of them, as Bella retired to her delightful little sitting room where she usually felt most comfortable. There she had all the materials to keep herself occupied, books, a stereo set, an old gramophone and hundreds of her favorite records, as well as any number of crafts materials that she so thoroughly enjoyed working with. This time though, she settled down with a pair of knitting needles and a skein of purple wool, but hadn't yet decided what she would produce. Her mood would direct the loops that would interconnect as her fingers would follow the shape of the product being produced.

Back in the ornate living room, Raphael was the one who did most of the speaking this time. And he had prepared himself with a lot of explanatory material.

Continuing on the subject where he had left off at the conclusion of their first meeting he continued, the third method of becoming Jewish involved the complex matter requiring a total modification to her personal status. She would have to undergo a change from being a free agent to that of legally selling herself into bondage. Though such a sale in itself is illegal it still is binding.

The Jewish Encyclopedia explains, the procedure in a simplified manner:[1]

The Bible requires the [non-Jewish] slave of a Jew to rest on the Sabbath and to observe the same commandments that any [Jewish] woman is obligated to observe. He can be released from his slavery either by being redeemed or by his master's freeing him by means of a document

---

[1] See appendix

to that effect. If the slave suffers any permanent injury to an organ (e.g., his eye or tooth) by the hand of his master, he is automatically granted the right to his freedom. Killing a Canaanite slave is considered to be murder. It is forbidden to return a runaway slave to his master (Devarim 23:16). Even though the Canaanite slave is formally the property of his owner, "it is pious and wise for a person to act mercifully and not to impose too heavy a burden on his slave and not to mistreat him, and to give him proper food and drink, and not to humiliate him by action or by word, and not to be excessively angry or to shout excessively, but to speak to him calmly and to hear his complaints" (*Shulchan Aruch, Yorai Daia* 267:17). A Canaanite slave who had been freed could become Jewish through immersion *(tevilah)* in a kosher mikvah and could then marry a Jew.

Voluntary manumission (granting of freedom) is not mentioned in the Torah, but the Talmud allowed masters to free slaves voluntarily by a number of mechanisms.[2]

Although, in their view, slave masters had previously had the right to revoke voluntary manumission, the classical rabbis instructed that it should no longer be permitted— (Talmud *Gittin* 1:6)

Other symbolic acts were also regarded as freeing the slave: namely, if the master put tephilin on the slave, gave him a free woman for a wife, or had him publicly read three or more verses from the Torah in public; if these acts were committed, it was compulsory for the master to give the former slave a writ of manumission (liberation from slavery).

It is very interesting to note that nearly every source quoted, regarding the Canaanite, or alien slave refers to the bondsman as a male. Hardly any source refers to the female slave. Meaning that putting tephilin on the female slave, having her publicly read three or more verses from the Torah definitely doesn't apply to the maidservant. What specific acts would have to be performed by a female slave in order for her to be eligible for manumission, if that was a requisite to becoming a free Jew?

One way would be to free her in order to have his son take her for a wife. In such a case, she would still probably be preparing the same meals and cleaning up after the same group of people that she had done as a slave. Might it not only free her from being enslaved to the master, only

---

[2]   see appendix

to have her immediately become enslaved, probably in the same house, to his son? That would all depend upon the personal relationship between the husband towards his wife.

If she were absolutely free, should she not be able to choose with which mate she prefers to share the rest of her life?

Or, as we mentioned earlier, the bondage of alien slaves could be terminated by payment of money, either by the slave or a third party. The sum probably, being the market value for a slave according to their age and physical attributes.

Another way that a slave would be emancipated (freed) would be if he or she would have been subject to a grievous bodily injury by their master in such a way that any one of the tips of his or her limbs were to bear a patent blemish resulting in any permanent disfigurement so that its original function does not return.[3] This does not include circumcision that must be preformed when the male slave is acquired, as being a necessary initiation rite to have him included in the master's household.

The injuries listed might be accidental, by negligence, purposely, or even inadvertently. The Talmud (Kedushin 24: b) relates a case whereby the slave of a master who was a practicing physician. He complained of an excruciating toothache, and asked his master to treat his ailing tooth. As soon as the tooth was extracted, the slave laughingly demanded a bond of emancipation. Even though the master was tricked into removing his tooth he was forced to free his slave.

Raphael continued, following receipt of a deed of release and emersion in a mikva the slave becomes a freeman or freewoman, and a full fledged Jew. They usually choose a Hebrew name for themselves, often considering themselves to be children of Avraham and Sarah. It is incumbent upon them to lead their lives in accord with Jewish practices, accepting all the obligations as laid down by Torah laws.

Willdo was overwhelmed by the lengthily exposition. Though it was expected that she would have many questions to ask, she seemed to be in a quandary, as to where to begin. However her first utterance was, "I know that at this time it seems premature, and probably silly, but I've already chosen a Hebrew name for myself, "Evatzaiyah"—an exact translation of

---

3   See appendix

135

Willdo. But if it's illegal to buy and sell slaves today in such a progressive country like Israel, how do we perform such a sale?

Raphael replied, "That seems to be the major problem to you, but it really isn't so difficult. We first must find someone who understands the situation and who would be willing to enter into such a transaction. The price to be paid would be in accord with the annual value of a laborer. So in reality it would be prepayment for services to be rendered during the next year. That can be explained as a perfectly legitimate transaction. The transfer of money must be made to the seller. That can be paid directly to you, who could deposit it into a bank account for safekeeping towards the time you might wish to purchase your freedom in the future. Of course you have a choice as to who would be your master or mistress. It would be more proper if you would be purchased by a woman, apropos the matter of modesty.

Setting up the contract of sale would have to be very carefully worded where in essence; you are to be totally subservient to your buyer's every wish and whim in accord with the sum of money paid for your unstinted services. You would have to immerse yourself in a kosher mikvah and become immediately obliged to abide by all the commandments incumbent upon a Jewish woman, including kashrut and Shabbat observance. A few additional points would have to be considered, but that would be the job of a lawyer to compose a binding contract, that would still be legally acceptable.

Bella, who has absented herself from their conversations, had no idea what was being discussed within the confines of her living room.

But Raphael thought that now was the time to include Bella in their deliberations, and called out, "Bella, can we have something to drink?"

Bella who had been knitting in her comfortable little sitting room across the hall replied, "Sure. I was wondering how long you could continue talking without even a sip of water to wet your lips." Within moments she entered the living room from the direction of the kitchen with a tray containing glasses and a pitcher of ice-cold water with a few slices of lemon floating on the surface. "If you want something hot, it will only take a few minutes to boil up some water." Raphael answered, "Thank you Bella, this is fine."

Then turning to Willdo, he apologetically asked, "Unless you wish to have something hot?"

Willdo replied, "No, thank you. I prefer cold water."

Raphael then turned toward Bella, once more and said, "Bella, will you sit down and join our discussion? I think that you might be of great help at this junction."

Raphael began by telling her, "We know that Willdo is too modest to deal with the Rabbinate in order to arrange for conversion. She was already rebuffed at her previous encounter with them, even though she realizes, that is the way they are supposed to react to prospective converts. To discourage them in order to weed out those who are not serious candidates. But their brusque manner turned her off completely.

He filled in Bella with the essence of his explanation about how Willdo would be able to fulfill her dream of becoming a fully dedicated Jewess. Then he asked her, "Bella, do you have any suggestions about how and with whom she could be sold into bondage?

Bella, who had not been present throughout the original session, was somewhat bewildered, if not shocked, at the thought of Willdo being sold into slavery, and yet to some stranger. They had lived together for some time already and understood each other in every respect. To even consider willingly sending Willdo out of her home was unthinkable.

"**Is** there no possibility of me buying her? After all, it is probably only a formality. This sale you're talking about. Is that not so?

Raphael replied, "Just as I thought. You wish to become her mistress/owner. I couldn't imagine it any other way. But you must be aware that your relationship would have to change. You'll have to forget about "Please and thank you". It will have to be "Do this and do that." You would have to put Willdo into her place if she should foul-up with some task.

"**Bella,** if you should agree to such a change," he continued, "Where do you stand financially? Could you pay her according to her value, equal to a whole year's salary, all in one lump sum?"

"**I** guess I might be able to dip into some savings, if I really had to. After all I usually make do with the income from my monthly pension."

And now turning to Willdo, he told her, "You'll have to make many changes in the way you relate to, and address Bella, especially before strangers. You'll be forbidden to call her by her name. It'll have to be 'Yes ma'am, and No ma'am," with a curtsy. Though you know and recognize the meat dishes from the dairy ones, you yourself will be prohibited from eating dairy foods till after six hours have passed from the time you ate any substance containing meat.

As for the Shabbat day, it's not that you'll be free of performing any labor only for Bella. But you will not be permitted to do any labor even for yourself. Not even to switch on any lights nor heat up water for a drink. Don't worry, you'll be properly instructed in due time as to what you will be permitted to do and prohibited from performing on Shabbatot and Festive days.

It you both agree to the idea, it would be advisable to find a lawyer who would understand the situation enough to draw up a legally binding deed of sale. It will have to be someone who is experienced in contracts yet knowledgeable in the fine aspects of Jewish law.

Bella excitedly broke in with, "My son Elhanan is a member of the bar. He specializes in drawing up contracts. Not only that, but he is now on a sabbatical from his law office, studying full time in a Yeshiva towards becoming a certified rabbi. I'm sure he would be the right man for the job. And I'm sure he would take a break from his studies for his mother's sake.

Raphael agreed that using her son's services would be ideal and asked Bella when she could contact her son Elhanan for an appointment.

The best time is when he's on a mealtime break. Otherwise his cell-phone is usually closed. So I can contact him in a couple of hours and explain the situation. I'll have him come for Shabbat and he could get all the information he needs to get started on Saturday night and if necessary, into Sunday.

Willdo was familiar with Elhanan already from the many times he came to visit his mother, and thought he would be the right person to entrust with such a project. Actually she knew no other lawyer in Israel.

Raphael stood up to take his leave with a promise to be in contact right after the end of Shabbat.

Somewhat after eight pm on this Wednesday night Elhanan heard his cell-phone jingle signaling that an incoming call was directed his way. It actually took him a few moments to remember in which pocket he had last placed his phone. He flipped it open and before he could acknowledge that he was prepared to take a call, he heard his mother's excited voice, "Elhanan. Elhanan. I don't care how busy you are but you must come for Shabbat. A situation has come up that only you can solve. I'm not even going to hint what it is because it would take too long and isn't that simple. I know you wish to study, and for that I admire your determination. But this is for a big *mitzvah*."

"**Okay** mom, With G-d's help, I'll be there on Friday afternoon. Is that all right?"

"**Fine,** Elhanan. I knew you wouldn't turn down my invitation. Don't worry, though, I feel fine and there's nothing to worry about. If it can wait till Shabbat, you can rest assured that I'm all right."

True to his word, Elhanan arrived on Friday afternoon. Willdo grabbed his satchel and before he could react to her speedy action she was already on her way to the laundry room with it.

This was not the first time she did his laundry when he arrived, but this time she was so thrilled at his arrival that without a word set to the task she was so used to.

The aura of this specific Shabbat was very much different from any other that he'd ever spent in his mother's house. The food seemed so special, the light seemed brighter, and the small talk and banter seemed so much more alluring than ever before. But no mention was made about the revolutionary changes that were about to take place within a very short time. Any which way the atmosphere could be kept placid, was realized. Eventually the day of rest drew to a close, and following the *havdalah*, marking the official change from the holiness of the Shabbat day to the irreverent days of the rest of the week.

The entire environment suddenly became intense. Not in any way depressing, but excitingly serious. That was when Bella first gave any indication of the changes that were to take place within her household. She told him, "Elhanan, you surely know Raphael. Don't you? The Talmid Hacham."

"**Yes,** I don't know him personally but know of his reputation of being an incredibly serious student, who leaves no stone unturned till he solves Talmudic problems. Why do you ask?"

"**Well** he's on his way here and should show up very soon. We have a very important proposal that includes your expertise as a lawyer."

"**Mom.** What kind of legal trouble did you get yourself into,? And what has that got to do with Raphael? I don't understand the connection. Mom, why didn't you tell me earlier? Surely we can work things out without getting strangers involved.

"**Brrrring!**" the front doorbell rang out. Willdo, who was already standing at the door, swung it wide open for the new arrival. Raphael strode right into the well lit living room.

"**Hi,** you must be Elhanan. My name is Raphael. I don't know how much you've been told, but as time is short, I suggest we settle down and let me start at the beginning.

Elhanan was somewhat perturbed at the way Raphael quickly took such a domineering lead of the proceedings in his mother's home. But he held back his annoyance, since his mother didn't seem to be irritated by it.

In less that five minutes Raphael ran through the essence of the problem and how he figured out how to solve the problem of Willdo's wish to become Jewish without reverting to the browbeating methods of the Rabbinate towards candidates for conversion. She was of too fine a character to be put through their grueling manners, and was too respectable to stoop to their level of insolence.

As Raphael continued explaining what steps were to be taken and how he anticipated the kind of contract that would be necessary in order to help Willdo achieve her goal, Elhanan realized the value of the groundwork that Raphael had done in preparation for this presentation. He gradually began to appreciate his analytic approach towards actualizing the plot. Raphael had left no stone unturned. All that he had to do was to draw up a legal document wherein his mother was to buy herself a slave and eventually free that slave so that she could bypass the Rabbinate's callous approach towards her becoming a full fledged Jewess. A simple but effective ruse.

Elhanan was getting caught up in the project with a growing enthusiasm that he hadn't experienced since completing his law degree thesis.

The basic contract form for such a purchase was straightforward.

However, one serious question remained to be thrashed out. Willdo wasn't comfortable about how to broach the subject, but it had to be discussed now. She began, "I still have one important question to ask.

Since I began working for Bella, I was earning a monthly wage, from which I was able to send money to my mother and father. They depend on my monthly contributions in order to survive. Should I become a slave without any cash income, how would I be able to help them out?

All three silently turned towards her. Neither one had any immediate reply to offer. This was one element that definitively had not been considered. Yet it was an important item in any agreement that they would enter. Willdo was to become a slave with dependants. This was a new twist that had to be regarded as serious, and required a just solution.

Bella then spoke up. "I realize how important that is to you as well as to your parents. And I'm certain we can work something out. Maybe Elhanan has a suggestion." Then turning to her son, added, "You'll surely know how it can be done, Elhanan." With that issue to be considered, the structure of the deed would have to include a special section about support of the slave's dependants.

Two kosher witnesses were arranged to be present, whereby they both witnessed writing up the deed of sale, and both signed individually and in sight of each other following the signatures of the seller and the buyer. both agreed that this date was most appropriate for their plot to be put into force.

Deed of Sale of a Slave

This contract, having been executed on the 15th day of the tenth month, namely Shevat in the year 5759,

On this day the functionary, Miss Willdo Waltin, twenty-three years of age, expressed the wish to sell herself into bondage as a slave to her former employer, Bella Baum. The price of has been fixed at thirty-six thousand New Israel Sheqels, to be deposited into a closed bank account for a minimum of one year with one stipulation, that the bank transfers the equivalent of two thousand New Israel Sheqels on the first day of each month for a period of twelve months, in the prevailing currency of Nepal, the Nepal Rupee to the account of Mr. Dado Waltin account in the Bank of Nepal.

The two parties to this contract have met face to face and have reached an agreement after joint discussions and an accord has been reached wherein at least one full year will have passed before any action is taken to have the slave manumitted by any accepted methods; either by cash payment of the slave's value or by the voluntary act of her mistress. In either case a writ of redemption would be legally drawn up and presented personally to the said slave.

The seller: Miss Willdo Waltin

The buyer: Mrs. Bella Blum

This deed of sale is duly witnessed and signed by:

Mr. Yitzhak Hoich

Mr. Yaacov Kurtz

One verbal stipulation by Raphael seemed to be somewhat odd to all those involved, but he promised that he would clarify its significance in due time. It was that Willdo, and nobody else, was to strike the match to light the havdalah candle every Saturday night.

The date chosen was to be on the New Year of the trees, as having been of special significance, ushering in the beginning of the spring season, when renewal is celebrated.

Since this was to be the beginning of a different kind of relationship between Willdo and Bella. They **During** the year beginning on Monday the 15th day of Shevat 5759 and ending on Friday the 14th day of Shevat 5760, Willdo's life as a slave was quite eventful. It was during this period of time that she learned much more than she had learned during the first twenty-three years of her life.

Her life as a slave had not been very different than it had been as a housemaid prior to that. Only now she had to be more careful about the stringencies of how a kosher household is managed. In addition to her being corrected from time to time about some seemingly odd intricacy like finding a dairy spoon in the meat cutlery drawer and how to go about koshering it.

While she had been a plain laborer, such minor occurrences didn't seem to make any difference to her. Bella always checked out the cutlery, and though she was warned about what to look out for, hadn't expected her to take upon herself any corrective action. But now it was her duty, in such a situation, to boil up a container of water and heat up a chunk of steel in order to kosher the stray spoon. She had to place it into the container of hot water and with a pair of tongs, maneuver the searing piece of steel into the same vessel, so that the resulting superheat would kosher the spoon. This was one of the innumerable ostensible infractions that could and did happen once in awhile. Every such problem had to be corrected as quickly as possible. The methods about how to handle these problems were sometimes much more complex, and had to be acquired.

However, if a dairy earthenware vessel had inadvertently come into contact with hot meat, there was no corrective action to take. It had to be scrapped, discarded, and thrown out.

She learned that the life of a Jew is not simple. In fact it can be quite complicated, but no one can claim it is not fascinating.

One of the most difficult things for her was learning to almost totally abstain from doing any labor during the entire Shabbat. I use the term "almost totally abstain" because certain situations would come up when some sort of loop-hole allows one to perform a labor of sort. For instance, tearing a leaf off a tree, or ripping a piece of paper is strictly forbidden, but when a sealed package of cookies have to be opened in order to eat from its contents, it is permissible to tear the wrappings, as long as any words printed on the wrapper are not torn.

Gradually Willdo, who was a willing student, became quite expert at knowing the ins and outs of Jewish Halacha within a few months.

It was a very exciting time for Willdo. She felt that she was nearly living a complete Jewish lifestyle, and towards the autumn, she was entrusted to prepare complete meals on her own, without supervision.

Elhanan had completed the tour of studies that would prepare him for the final exams towards his being a certified Rabbi. Willdo was included in the planning stages of the feast in celebration of that event. It would be attended by the strictest rabbis of the entire community and the kashrut had to be with the utmost stringency. No questionable item would be tolerated, under any circumstances. Several additional ultra-religious cooks and aids were hired, but Willdo was to supervise the entire project. She was in it from the planning stages, through the shopping, preparation, storage, and serving the foods. And it all went with clockwork. She was involved in every aspect of her supervisory position except handling the wines, as she was still not Jewish.

Actually she didn't realize that all eyes of the hired help were following her every move in order to ascertain that she made no mistakes, and she passed the test with flying colors.

After Elhanan was granted his certificate as a full fledged Rabbi he was addressed as Rabbi Elhanan or Rabbi Blum, he was at home much of the time, even though he now had a teaching position.

Willdo suspected that some secret plans were being laid, because whenever she came close to members of the household, durable silence would suddenly fall between them till she would be out of hearing range.

These loud silences supported her suspicions, but she hadn't known how far the secret discussions had progressed and how much she would be affected by them.

Winter came and the month of Shevat was quickly approaching. She had so become used to the slave/mistress relationship between Bella and herself that she even forgot that nearly one full year had passed since she sold her freedom and became a slave nearly one year ago.

A long time had passed since she had last seen Raphael, when he suddenly appeared for a short visit. Hardly a word, other than a Shalom upon his arrival and his departure passed between them. His stay was altogether curt and he was soon on his way again. Something strange was going on in this house, and she wasn't in on the secret. It began to disturb her no end.

Then on Thursday morning, the thirteenth day of Shevat, Willdo was called into the living room and told to get her coat and be prepared to leave within a few moments. She did as she bidden, and after a short trip was ushered out of the car and directed into a bridal salon, where she was invited to try on several gowns. From there it became a shopping spree for other clothing, shoes and accessories to match. **Nobody** asked her. She was just being told. After all she was a slave and nobody asks a slave.

One is told and one does as one is directed.

The very next day, Friday was spent as any other Friday, preparing for the advent of Shabbat.

Bella's daughter Debbie, who she had never yet met, her husband and their three children, arrived from the other side of the continent to join them to celebrate this Shabbat.

As soon as Shabbat was over and the havdalah was recited she was ushered into the family living room and was presented with a note that read:

Willdo was advised to be prepared for the next step. She was to be accompanied to the mikvah to complete the process of becoming a Jew, as well as in preparation for her wedding. This was too much to absorb simultaneously.

Deed of Manumission

On this date the 15th day of the tenth month, namely Shevat in the year 5760, Miss Willdo Waltin, who had served as a slave to Mrs. Bella Blum since the 15th day of Shevat 5759, is now manumitted.

She is, of this date, a freewoman and can of her own choosing live her life as a Jewess.

This manumission is hereby granted her as a gift with no strings attached.

However she is being asked to consider a proposal of marriage to the son of Mrs. Bella Blum, namely the eminent Rabbi Elhanan Blum, which can take place immediately, upon her acceptance of this deed of manumission.

Signed this date, the 16th day of Shevat 5760
Owner: Mrs. Bella Blum
Witness: Mr. Yitzhak Hoich
Witness: Mr. Yaacov Kurtz

She hardly slept a wink all night, while thoughts were swelling up in her mind. If she though this was a surprise, she had no idea what real astonishment awaited her. Her being a freewoman, and a full fledged Jew was nearly too much for her to grasp at one time.

Sunday morning began early and she was in a complete daze while being led around to a beauty parlor, then to have her wedding gown final fitting, being primped and served from all directions with no time to really reflect upon her new status. She had to remind herself about who she really was, as the day wore on.

Early in the afternoon she was told to be prepared for a make-up session that included manicure and pedicure treatments, then she was dressed up in her satin wedding gown. The one she'd tried on a couple of days before, was given a last minute make-up treatment, and was whisked away in a comfortably large car to a wedding hall. **Without** realizing what was happening, she suddenly become conscious of the fact that she hadn't seen Rabbi Elhanan since Friday. He had spent the entire Shabbat with some friends.

That is one of the traditions with a Jewish wedding. The bride and groom don't see each other for the entire day of the wedding, till he checks to see if she is really the bride before covering her face with a veil.

Evatzaiyah slowly made her way up the wide stone stairs towards the entrance of the hall, accompanied by two young girls, on either side of her, when she suddenly stopped in shock. Through the plate glass window, a pair of eyes she hadn't seen in some years peered directly at her. No! It couldn't be. But it was just so. It was nobody other than her mother, Momba. What was Momba doing here? How in the world did she ever arrive here? And Dado, her father gazed at her through the glass door. "What's going on here?" She asked herself. After all the excitement throughout the entire day, this was too much to comprehend.

She ran ahead of her bridesmaids and threw open the door and with all her strength embraced both her mother and father together. Unrestrained tears intermingled and coursed down their cheeks unchecked, streaking her make-up. They didn't release each other for a long time. She finally found her voice and asked them, "How did you know where and when to come?"

This was the result of another one of Bella's behind the scenes secrets. She had contacted Willdo's parents, after explaining to the bank manager why it was necessary for her to have their address, and had them flown over just three days before the planned wedding of their daughter. Her parents were set-up in a hotel to be kept out of Willdo's sight till this very moment.

The rest of the ceremony was like a dream. She hardly remembered what questions she was asked, and how she replied to them. But one thing for sure, when she was asked what name was to be entered on the official documents she immediately replied, "Evatzaiyah daughter of Avraham and Sarah."

Evatzaiyah stood under the canopy beside Rabbi Elhanan, but her eyes swept over her parents most of the time.

After the bride had taken a sip from the second cup of wine Raphael, who was one of the two *shashbanim* asked, "Well Evatzaiyah how do you feel now? Evatzaiyah, wearing her satiny white wedding gown, and after having had her veil thrust back to reveal her cheerful face, now occupied with transferring her wedding band from her index finger to the ring finger excitedly replied, "Just one year ago I was a common *shiksah* and now, I'm an honored *Rebbitzin!*"

Just then the entire hall was filled with a reverberating sound as the groom's right foot came crashing down to purposely smash a glass, **Thunkrashhhh!!**

EPILOGUE

Later on that evening; Bella, Raphael, Rabbi Elhanan and Evatzaiyah found themselves together, but separated from the rest of the crowd, when Evatzaiyah spoke up, "Rav Raphael, I dutifully followed your explicit instructions for the entire year, about my striking the match used in lighting the havdalah candle on Saturday nights, but still have no idea why it always had to be me. You promised that you would eventually explain the reason. Don't you think that it's about time you told us?"

With a smile on his lips, showing pleasure in her remembering to ask, he began. "A non-Israelite is prohibited from observing the Jewish Shabbat. And one who inadvertently does so is guilty of violating a decree that is punishable by death. While you were obligated to observe all commandments incumbent upon a Jewish woman, you were still not a Jewess yet. Therefore you had to perform some kind of act that would be prohibited. And since the day for Jews begins at dusk and ends with the following nightfall. A Jew would be allowed to strike that match after dark on Saturday night. However the day of an alien begins and ends at midnight.

"By your striking that match, you performed an act prohibited on *your* Shabbat. Therefore by your sinful act you were absolved of the more stringent ruling that is punishable by death, that of keeping the Jewish Shabbat by a non-Jew."

"From now on, however, you would be performing a worthy act by striking the match, but you would first have to utter the short blessing, Haamavdil bein kodesh lichol.

APPENDIX TO BECOMING JEWISH

1 A Canaanite slave is the property of his master and is bought for all time. He does not go free in the jubilee year. The Torah states, *"Such male and female slaves as you may have—it is from the nations round about you that you may acquire male and female slaves . . . These shall become your property. You may keep them for a possession for your children after you, for them to inherit for all time. Such you may treat as slaves"* (Vayikra 25:44-46).

However, even the life of the Canaanite slave is not totally under the master's control. Once the slave is circumcised, he is considered to be a member of the family and he partakes of the paschal sacrifice together with everyone else. In fact if an alien slave is not circumcised he prevents the rest of his master's family from partaking of the Pascal lamb on the night of Pessach, as taught by Rambam.

2. Such manumission was to be formally executed by a written deed (the *shetar shihrur*), which must sever the dependency and servitude completely; if any of the master's *rights* were reserved, or the deed was written in the future tense, it would be invalid and ineffectual. These deeds would become effective as soon as it was transferred to a 3rd party, or delivered to the slave; however, if the master had sent the deed to the slave, it would become void if the master died before the slave received it. Possession of the deed was counted as <u>prima facie</u> proof of manumission, but the former slave was not allowed to work on land gifted to him by his former master, unless witnesses were able to verify the valid transfer as a gift. Despite the general disregard for non-Jewish laws, writs of manumission written by non-Jewish magistrates were acknowledged to retain their validity under Jewish law. [from Mishneh Torah, and from *Gittin* 1:4 (<u>Tosefta</u>)]

Indeed, if the master merely says that he has freed his slave, the rabbis would not even allow him to repudiate his statement, instead compelling such a master to create a writ of manumission—*Gittin* 40b even if the slave denies that he has been given this writ, he is still considered freed—"Gittin 40b"

In Rambam's opinion, manumission could not even be carried out by wills; this, however, was a technicality, as Maimonides still permits heirs themselves to be compelled by a will to carry out manumission of the deceased owner's slaves.

The Bible said, a slave should be freed if they had been harmed to the extent that their injury was covered by the lex talionis—Shemot 21:26-27, should actually only apply to slaves who had converted to Judaism; additionally, Rambam argues that this manumission was really punishment of the owner, and therefore that it could only be imposed by a court, and required evidence from witnesses.—

3. This is based upon the passage in the Torah, *"And if a man smite the eye of his servant, or the eye of his maid, and destroy it; he shall let him go free for his eye's sake. And if he smite out his manservant's tooth, or his maidservant's tooth; he shall let him go free for his tooth's sake."* (Shemot 21: 26-27). According to the Talmud, the mention of the eye or the tooth is a generalization relating to any of the projecting limbs. (Fingers, toes, ears, nose, membrum or nipples).